I CAME TO PLAY YOUR GAME

I CAME TO PLAY YOUR GAME

A talent from beyond sees football and life through a different lens

CRAIG GARNER

I CAME TO PLAY YOUR GAME

A talent from beyond sees football and life through a different lens

by Craig Garner

First Edition
Copyright © 2025 by Craig Garner

Published by
Munn Avenue Press
300 Main Street, Ste 21
Madison, NJ 07940
MunnAvenuePress.com

Paperback ISBN: 978-1-969679-17-9
Hardcover ISBN: 978-1-969679-18-6

Printed in the United States of America

To Peg, for 55 years
of love and patience.

CONTENTS

PART ONE

Arrival

1

I CAREFULLY WATCHED THE GAME FOR A WEEK. I LOVED THE SPEED, collisions, the loud voice yelling numbers, checks and signals at a boy nestling the ball between his legs. It was what I had come for, what I had been sent to learn and adapt to.

After studying a full scrimmage, I decided I was ready. I asked the man with the whistle if I could play.

"You go to Cascades?" he asked. "I ain't seen you before."

"You mean over there?" I pointed to the building beyond the fence.

"Yeah, you a student or what?"

The man talked without turning. He didn't seem all that impressed with someone admiring the game he was supervising. He just wanted to know where I came from as if that was all that mattered.

"I am new to these parts. If I go to the building and tell them who I am, can I participate on this team of yours?"

"That would be about right."

"Well, then I shall be back."

"Bring a piece of paper saying you're registered. Get your parents to sign permission for you to play too."

I nodded. If that's all it takes, I was sure I could generate official-looking documents that would get me through the gate and onto that wide green field.

"You're tall all right." He finally glanced my way. "But a little gawky. Actually, you look downright strange in the light you're standing in."

"I don't believe it will matter once I join the rest."

The man with the whistle had broad shoulders, a blocky head, a stomach that plowed over his belt. To me, *he* looked strange compared to all the others who were young and strong in yellow shorts, blue shirts, and hard hats to protect their heads.

"Whaddaya play?" he asked.

"That game you're teaching. Could learn it pretty fast, I expect."

"I mean position."

"I can run as well as any of your pledges. Faster probably. And that ball you throw around, I can catch even though it looks disproportionately shaped."

"Disproportionate? What, are you in STEM?"

"I don't know what that is... but I can adjust to the level of what's required."

"I'm asking where should I try you?" The man wore a cap, but it didn't protect his facial skin much. It was blotchy red and unevenly shaved.

"You may place me anywhere, depending on your needs."

"Yo, I need playmakers. Got any of that in you?"

"We should find out, shouldn't we?"

✶ ✶ ✶

I went to the building the next day. Once I slipped past the guard at the front entrance, I found myself in a brightly lit, centrally located office.

I approached an erect, serious woman at the front desk. "I'd like a paper that says I can play the game on the big field that's inside the large seating arena," I told her.

"You mean football?"

"Yes, that's my singular objective. To become one of the boys in yellow shorts and hard headgear with pictures of horns on them."

"You a student? What grade are you in?"

"I could be. I'm new to this region."

The woman flipped some glasses down off her forehead. She squinted behind the lenses.

"New, heh? You're unusual-looking, ears sorta notched. What part of the Cascades you living in?"

"Over near the Golden Arches. We just moved in." I had seen them on my way to the field. Two glowing spans that cars drove under and people entered to consume food.

"You talking about McDonald's? There are a few of them around."

"I'm new, as I say. I reside near the Gates of Wisdom Forest."

"You sure that's in our district?" The woman was vigilant, not about to be made a fool of. "I've got better things to do than make sense of strangers."

A man suddenly came out of a door and called to her. He must have been important. She left me to go see him immediately.

I took the opportunity to search the papers scattered on the counter. I found some that looked official. They had CALLISTER CASCADES HIGH SCHOOL stamped at the top with a printed picture of an animal with horns next to the lettering. They looked like the horns the boys on the field had on their hard hats.

I swiped a few of the papers and shoved them in my waistband.

When the woman returned, she asked my age and if I had any transfer papers from my previous school.

I had to think fast. It's why I had been sent.

"I'm sixteen. My papers got destroyed in a fire."

"So, you've got no records? To show what grade you might be entering?"

"No, ma'am." I was always taught that politeness got you far.

"Okay, I'm going to assign you to Mr. Fasciola's homeroom. Eleventh grade. Good place for the odd types we can't categorize."

* * *

I gave Mr. Sawyer—he said to call him "Coach"—the papers the next day. I'd filled in the pertinent information the night before with the help of the Emissary.

"So, it says you're a—ahhh—Keysian. What in blazes is that?"

"We emigrated here to the forests out by the Gates of Wisdom."

"Okay, okay . . . don't care where you're from long as you can play."

Coach took a stab at examining my papers. "These grades on your transcript . . . all As in trigonometry, botany, classical literature, music composition. You sure you're not looking for the debate team instead of football?"

Our Emissary had also forged a B in programming and a C in digital art just so I appeared normal.

"Go find the equipment managers in the locker room. They'll suit you up."

I had some trouble with the shoulder pads, fitting them to my sloping shoulders. The hard hat they gave me was called a helmet, I soon learned. And cushions tucked inside my shorts so I "didn't lose my manhood" kept popping loose.

When I took the field, Coach lined me up with the pass-catchers.

He winked. "You look sort of lean and slippery in a funky kinda way."

I stood in a line behind the others and watched. They ran so many steps down the field, turned quickly, and held up their hands at the spherical ball sailing toward them. The purpose was to catch it, spin, and dash away from the bodies trying to stop them.

First time I ran the turn-and-catch route, the ball hit me between the face mask and helmet brim, and stuck. I turned to run but couldn't, the lodged ball blocked my vision. All the other pass-catchers around me fell on the ground laughing.

Second time I caught the ball with both hands like the others.

Third time, I snagged it with one hand and ran a circle around my defender. I heard nothing but whistles and "Whoa, bro, shake it."

I copied everything the pass-catchers did. Long runs and difficult catches over their shoulders. Short darting grabs over the middle of the field. Running in motion behind what the coach called the line of scrimmage. You were also supposed to crash into a body across from you when the player on our side was carrying the ball.

I only had to watch once and I immediately absorbed the intent of each activity. Once, I caught a pass and slung the ball behind me to one of my teammates following me downfield.

"STOP!" Coach yelled. "Where in tarnation you learn that?"

"It just felt right," I explained. "Not as many defenders were around him as were around me."

"Shit, kid, you don't get to flip the ball around like it's a loose lugnut."

Coach shook his head at some other maneuvers he did not approve of.

I caught a pass out of bounds and ran untouched all the way to the scoring zone. I did three straight somersaults to get free instead of just running what he called a "pattern." I took a handoff from the ball handler—I learned he was called the quarterback—and tossed it back blindly over my head to him when defenders closed in on me. He ran for what quickly became known to me as a "touchdown," the most crucial goal of any football game.

After my first practice, Coach Sawyer asked me where I'd learned to play.

I didn't want to tell him the truth. This was the first day I had ever played.

"Well, it seems you got a lot of renegade in you. You ain't bound by the laws other people play this game."

"I admit I get caught up in extemporaneous invention."

"Eh, yeah." Coach clapped me on my shoulder pads. "You don't talk that way with the other guys, do you?"

"I don't know. I am meeting them for the first time."

"Word of advice," Coach winked. "I'd rein it in."

"Thanks, Coach Sawyer, I appreciate you guiding me along the correct path."

He took off his cap and waved it in front of his face. "You're either a breath of fresh air or you're putting me on."

To match his gesture, I removed my helmet with the curling horns. "I will put you on, sir, as I advance each day with my improved play."

Coach rolled his eyes and left the field with a shrug.

2

The next morning, I reported to Mr. Fasciola's room after conferring with the Emissary. He advised that I abide by the rules of the Callister Cascades School District. The other students in the class stared at me. I thought they might be curious because it was the first day I'd ever been in their midst. One boy with a mountainous tuft of hair growing straight up asked if I was in the right place.

"The authority in the main office sent me here," I answered.

"Probably didn't know what to do with you. We're sort of the school's mongrels."

"I play football," I said, fumbling to make conversation.

"I do too," replied Big Hair.

"Yesterday was my first day."

"I've been playing forever. But this year really looks even better. The player ratings are going to change throughout the game, and the passing mechanics are going to be even sharper on the screen."

I didn't want to appear dense. So, I said, "Yes, the middle screens Coach showed us with the lead blockers, it'll make us a lot of yardage."

"We talking the same thing?" said Big Hair.

"Aren't you on the field with Coach Sawyer?"

"You kidding? That's like sweating and grunting. I'm talking about playing *College Football 25* on PlayStation. Be at least fifty of us in the Cascades Game

Hall on the desktops after school."

"Oh," I said. "I'm talking about the real thing."

"That is the real thing," he said, his hair standing even more rigid. "I'm going to play solo challenges across consoles, build the Ultimate Team, and run the Champs Gauntlet."

I was prepared, of course, to understand why my fellow students were dependent on electronic devices, lighted screens, and faceless interaction with each other. I deduced he was talking about electronic games. I wished Big Hair the best of luck and suggested that maybe he venture out into the fresh air and watch some real football every so often.

He smiled and we slapped hands above our heads.

"Yeah, keep it real," Big Hair cheered.

I had made my first friend.

*　*　*

When I met my homeroom teacher, Mr. Fasciola, he naturally wanted to know my name. I had been told to keep it simple. Walker or James or Freeman. I can't tell you why; I just felt rebellious. I blurted Sublimious Z. Hormats.

"That's rather grandiose." He was a big man with an imposing black beard.

I knew immediately I'd made a mistake. "But you can call me Clancy," I corrected.

He was jotting essential information in a notebook. "Clancy, huh. I liked the first one, Sublimious. Where's that come from?"

"It's derived from 'sublime,' meaning splendid or noble. But I don't wish to stand out in here, in your class. I intend to impress on the football field."

Mr. Fasciola stopped writing in his notebook and inspected me with a sharp eye. "Well, that's an admirable ambition, I guess. But you don't look like any kind of special athlete. You're tall but don't appear particularly muscular."

"I can assure you that coordination, determination and ingenuity will clearly give me an advantage. My looks may even lull the opposition into a less than vigilant state."

Mr. Fasciola sat back, crossed his legs and stroked his chin. "You're very confident, aren't you? I'm surprised they stuck you in my homeroom. They usually send me the incorrigibles."

"I can only tell you that the front desk thought you might have a salubrious effect on me." I sat back and beamed at my hyperbole.

"I doubt that, Sublimious. They were just trying to shuffle you out the door."

"Nevertheless, I'm glad to be in your presence. I expect you will help give me an educational sheen that will allow my football prowess to flower."

Mr. Fasciola stood and tucked away his notebook. "I don't know where you come from, but you might expand your horizons. Football is but one facet of a well-rounded individual. This school isn't known for its gridiron prowess."

"I can assure you, sir, I am not one-dimensional."

*　*　*

I sat next to a girl in homeroom. I had studied American girls in preparation for my extended visit. They were slimmer than boys and less physically developed from a muscular standpoint. However, they were said to surpass boys in emotional maturity and their ability at accommodation.

I must admit the first girl I met did not fit the categories I just mentioned.

She wore a heavy shirt with the image of a fist striking an object and the word "POW" above it emblazoned in a vivid crimson. A tight short skirt revealed hard-coiled legs tucked into fringed leather work boots.

"What're you staring at?" she said in a raspy tone.

I fumbled for an answer. "Your hair—I like it." It did not stick straight up like the first boy I met. Hers looked as if it had undergone an explosive blond electric shock.

"You mocking me or something?"

"Oh, no, I think it complements your oval face perfectly."

"Oval? What's oval about it?"

"It's radiance. Isn't an oval a gem?"

"That's opal, you idiot."

"Oh, sorry, sometimes I have real elucidation issues."

"Yeah, I'd say you got more than that."

She was chewing something. I had heard of cud. But I did not think it was cud because she blew a bubble and popped it.

I leaned back and reevaluated. "Are you a cheerleader? I play football, and I understand the players have devotees on the sidelines who cheer them on."

The girl punched her electronic device shut in her hand. "Do I look like the cheerleader type?"

"I can't tell. I haven't had a chance to study them that closely."

"Well, when you do, you'll find I don't fit the standard mold."

I was gratified. At least a girl was talking with me.

"I'm new," I said. "Would you mind if we exchanged names?"

"Sam. Sam the Slam. You seen my shirt?"

"Yes, it's a very, ahh... very resounding image."

"Resounding, hell. I can mash heads when I gotta."

"Yes, I think that shirt sends the message."

"Damn straight," Sam growled.

"You know I'm aware that women are breaking all sorts of 'glass ceilings,' I think they call it. Could you play football? You seem to have the right attitude."

Sam leaned back in her seat and propped one sinewy leg up against the desk. "Maybe gave it a thought once or twice. But I don't think this school's ready for that kind of breakthrough."

"Tomorrow," I said, "when I see Coach Sawyer, I could put in a good word for you. He'd like that electric bush-cut of yours. You wouldn't even need a helmet."

Sam laughed and kicked off her boots. A pungent smell floated up.

"You know you're not like most guys in this class. They won't even talk to me. I'm like in my own depraved world to them. You... you don't seem to care."

"I'm sampling everyone here for the first time," I replied. "I think you're *quintessential*." I was experimenting with a word I rather liked for its elegance.

"Whoa, if that's dirty, I don't really mind."

I extended a hand and we shook. "I'm Sublimious Z. Hormats, but you can call me Clancy if you prefer."

"Sam . . . Samantha Schneider. Slam if I gotta work out of trouble."

Sam had a grip that sent a shiver through my entire arm.

Without much calculation, I had made a second friend.

3

For the next week, I became part of the Callister Cascades Rams. I put on my warm-ups and showered in the same dressing room, did calisthenics and wind sprints on the auxiliary fields next to the stadium, listened to the wisdom of Coach Sawyer when we gathered on one knee in circles around his autocratic countenance.

"Boys, I'm proud of the way you came out this season and got back in the grind with real piss and vinegar. Them teams in our conference takin' us for granted again this year. Think they can beat us with one hand tied behind their backs. But we're gonna shock the living bejesus out of 'em, aren't we?"

I heard a buzz around me, sort of like the buzz wasps make while flitting around on the undersides of the football stadium seats.

"We're gettin' in the best shape of our lives, so in the fourth quarter when the game's on the line, we'll roll over 'em like a two-ton Mack truck haulin' wet cement."

Again, a hum, but this time more like flies stuck inside a closed classroom.

Afterward, I asked my pass-catcher colleagues if they were inspired by Coach Sawyer's oration.

"Aw, it's the same ol' jack every year."

"'Cept I never heard the truck hauling wet cement thing before."

"Yeah, last year we were a drone droppin' bunker-buster bombs."

I, of course, being a novice, was impressed that a band of seventy or so boys got together every day after class to sweat, exercise and drill for the upcoming season of ten or eleven games.

The guys I spent most time with were the ones who ran down the field and had the leather ball thrown to them. Their names were Aurelius, Styles, Kadeem, Heath and a tall reddish-brown kid, Ladarius, who said I could be his workout partner. That was important because I had a lot to learn.

He showed me how to lift weights and do bench presses and agonizing squats in this odiferous room without windows. We'd go outside, even in the rain, and do hurdle drills, shuttle runs and 40-yard dashes. I loved the box blasts where we jump on and off a three-foot-high crate.

Ladarius said I ran a 3.9-second 40-yard dash. He kept shaking his stopwatch. "This gotta be wrong," he said. "Nobody's ever run that fast."

"I should perhaps run it backward," I suggested.

"Look, I don't think you're trying to show your ass off," he advised. "But you're blowin' guys away and you act like it's nothin'."

"I could run it sideways," I said. "I sort of like it when we glide and swiggle along like a duck in a pond."

"Since when you been watchin' ducks?"

"I try to copy animals since I believe they understand how to cut down on air resistance much better than we do as... ah, humans."

"Jesus, you know, Sublimious, you say the damnedest things."

"Since you are a friend, you can call me Clancy."

When we lined up to run pass routes, Ladarius gave me a nudge. "Don't do spins or cartwheels on your defender," he advised. "That's posin' or show-boatin.' You can get your head taken off if the guy thinks you're making a mark out of him."

I listened to Ladarius. He had my best interests in mind. However, my problem was that I ran faster than anybody on the team. Faster than Coach Sawyer had ever seen. "You got some secret ignition, Clancy?" he'd ask. "You run like the wind. Just don't wave your hands when you're open by twenty yards."

I was forever indebted to my mentors for enhancing my behavior.

The quarterback, whose name was Prince as in royalty, whispered a play to me. "Look, line up beside me and then start walking with a limp toward the side-lines. Pulled hamstring or something. Then almost keel over like you need the help of the trainer. When everybody sluffs off you, take off like a bat out of hell, and I'll hit you in the back of the endzone."

I thanked him for having faith in me. I really embellished my "injury" for all it was worth. Suddenly, I took off and caught his bullet aerial as I broke wide open.

Our defensive safety came over to me and slugged me hard in the chest. "You work that again and they'll find you clawin' for air inside a body bag."

Prince looked over and grinned. I believe I had been what is called *suckered*.

* * *

Ladarius took me to a little café in downtown Callister Cascades called Drakos. It was owned by his father, Nico, who cut an imposing figure in a food-spattered apron.

"You're the new kid," said Big Nico. That was what Ladarius called him, *Big Nico*. "Word is you run like you're shot from a cannon. Maybe you and Lad can bookend the team this year and win more than two or three games finally."

"We plan to be spectacularly successful," I nodded.

Big Nico's heavy eyebrows lifted. "Yeah, well, good to hear."

"Order whatever you want," he said. "Lad knows the menu."

Ladarius was calm, confident. He explained that his father was Greek, his mother was African American, and that they didn't live together anymore.

"I'll get Dad to bring us gyros and a spinach pie. Don't know what you eat at home, but you'll like it, I guarantee."

I refrained from telling him what I ate at home or where I lived. I did want to hear about the "rules of the road" that Ladarius promised to share with me, so I sat with my hands folded in the blue and white checkered booth. Ladarius said they were the colors of the Greek flag.

"You been practicin' with us, what, more than three weeks now?" he began.

"You're good. You know you're good. We all *really* know you're good. But, man, you do some crazy-ass stuff. Like running routes in curlicues. Doing spins and somersaults off the line. That deal where you hide behind the goalpost and jump out like some kind of Halloween skeleton. The other guys look at you like you don't got a whole lot of respect for the game... or for them."

I was startled and displeased to hear this. I had been told by my Oracle that American football was an exercise in creativity and originality.

Now I was being told that "I stuck out like a loose nail and most of the team was going to hammer me in." That was the way Ladarius put it.

"I wish to understand the purpose of this game, what we as pass catchers are expected to do," I said. "You know, the absolute untrammeled objective."

Ladarius leaned back, a thoughtful look on his face. "With us wide receivers, it is to get open. It is to find creases in the zones and breakdowns in man-to-man coverage. It is to move the first-down chains. *Numero uno*, it is to put the ball in the endzone at least one more time than the other team."

"I thought so," I replied. "I've become dubious that I've interpreted the rules wrong."

"Yeah, but Sublimious, the rules I'm talking about are how you go about getting that done. You can soar like an eagle, but you have to do it within the confines of the team. You don't flap and yammer and preen like some peacock on speed."

Big Nico brought us what he called a gyro and a flaky square of spinach and cheese pie. *Spanakopita*, he called the pie. He set hot cups of tea in front of us and spooned in three helpings of sugar before I could say, "No, thank you."

"That'll make you run even faster," he said. "I want to see Lad on a team that deals some hurt to the bobos who been stompin' us in the past."

"Well, sir, we will each contribute our fair share to steady improvement."

The large man placed both hands on the tabletop. I could see where his son got his quiet power. "You came to us at the right time," he said to me in his deep voice. "Don't know where you came from or how you got here, neither does Lad. But he tells me he thinks it's a gift from the football gods who know how to make the world turn like it's finally intended."

"Yessir, your son is most helpful. Otherwise, I could be a peacock, and you know what happens to them when they try to fly in their non-aerodynamic bodies."

Mr. Drakos gave me an odd grin. I don't think he quite understood my adage. I'm not sure I understood it myself.

* * *

We had our first scrimmage game against Whitaker Catholic from the next town over. It wasn't to count in the regular season. "Just to see how far we come or how far we still got to go," Coach Sawyer told us.

This team was *baaaad*, Ladarius warned. As in the type that would take pleasure in annihilating us and leaving us for dead. Ladarius took me aside and gave me a quick refresher of his rules of the road: Play within the confines of the game plan. No ballet dancer pirouettes or flamenco whirligigs. You can make amazing plays without having to put the cherry on top.

He cooly told me I had to fit in without rubbing it in.

I had conferred with the Emissary. He was quite adamant. ***You must listen to your friend. He is telling you not to go beyond the traditional football boundaries. If you do you will become a pariah and not be able to absorb the knowledge from the game as we seek it.***

I must pull in my horns, so to speak. That was not an easy thing to do for an energetic young Keysian explorer or a Callister Cascades Ram.

So, when Coach Sawyer finally put me in in the second quarter, I had to keep my poise as I confronted the Whitaker *Whoop-asses*. That's what they called themselves.

The defender across from me had eye black painted down his cheeks in the shape of sharpened sword blades. His mouth curled in an angry snarl. He growled that he was going to break me into fifty pieces.

Quite honestly, I thought he could if he ever got hold of me. I told myself that he never would.

I ran directly at him, juked right, and pivoted back to the center of the field, running what Coach called a "Z route." I left his *whooped ass* in a cloud of dust. Prince hit me with a perfect spiral, and I sprinted to the "Promised Land."

Ladarius ran into the endzone to make sure I behaved. "No celebratin'!" he hollered. "No full-body flips, no cartwheels. Just hand the ball to the ref like good ol' respectful Sublimious."

I did as I was told. I actually bowed to the official.

As I passed Coach Sawyer on the way to the bench, he was beaming ear to ear. "Clancy, you got turbojets in them feet of yours?"

"Coach," I joyfully answered, "I am simply running the patterns you so ably taught me."

He screwed up his stubbly face. "You puttin' me on again?"

"No, sir, you line me up on the other side and I will duplicate the soaring tactics that you have drilled into my whole being."

Coach didn't usually listen to my inexperienced chatter. This time he did.

I lined up opposite a player who looked even stronger and meaner than Sword Blade. As I broke straight at him, he elbowed me to make sure I got his unmistakable message.

I hunched over to pretend he had hurt me. Then I unlimbered and turned on Coach's turbojets. I remember seeing my defender twenty yards in my rear-view mirror. He was shaking his fist and yelling silent words. Prince laid the ball in my hands like a precious egg.

After the scrimmage finished, the Whitaker coach sought me out. "Hey, did some mad scientist put you together in a laboratory?" he asked quite seriously. "I haven't seen a receiver leave my corners in puddles on two straight plays like you done. Your speed's ungodly."

I only smiled. That was what the Emissary would have counseled me to do.

Ladarious came over and slapped my shoulder pads. "You bought into the rules. I'm proud of you. You weren't the preening peacock I feared you might be."

I laughed, of course, and suggested we go to his dad's café for gyros. He didn't realize how much self-discipline it took for me to play this game in a no-frills straitjacket.

Prince and the rest of the Rams threw me into the showers while I was still wearing my uniform. I thought it was a sign of acceptance.

4

The Emissary communicated with me in a small, secluded safe house in the most isolated part of the Gates of Wisdom Forest. I went there when beckoned. Otherwise, I stayed in a cottage registered to my grandfather. I told nobody where I lived, not even my new best friend Ladarious Drakos.

I had to be ready when called by the Emissary. The safe house was hidden amid tall trees. I would go and sit in a hard-backed chair in an empty room as I waited. Suddenly the voice of the Emissary seemed to issue from the walls and ceiling in a mellow, inquisitive tone: *Do you think your assignment to learn and play American football will ultimately benefit us Keysians if we ever have to resettle in this distant land?*

"I hope so, your Excellency. It is a game that suits the land and its people. We must understand it thoroughly. I have found a sound guide who does not ask too many questions."

That is good. We do not wish to have our motives readily decoded.

"I know," I sighed. "I have been told to pull in my horns so that I do not become a loose nail that has to be pounded in. That image is puzzling to me. I cannot picture my teammates pounding me into a hard board."

When the Emissary laughed, he sounded like a bass drum. *Boo-woom!*

You do not have an easy assignment. None of our explorers do. Just think of the one we sent to be an entrepreneur in the American capitalist system. The politicians want to regulate him, and his investors want to know how fast he can reach their outrageous demands for a high return on capital.

"Yes." I sat back in my plain chair. "All I have to do is use my ungodly Keysian speed. That's what my coaches call it. Their gods are not like ours."

The Emissary often paused before he spoke. Sometimes when he cleared his throat, it sounded like overhead beams cracking.

Sublimious, you have to understand why we chose to focus on football. It pervades American society seven months out of their year. Many are consumed by it totally. They bet their weekly and monthly wages on it. Everyone from children to old men walk around wearing their team logo and colorful jerseys.

"I am learning, sire. I think it was wise that the Powers sent me to an American high school that has not always had a successful sports record. As we improve, we will see how it affects the school, the students, the town—"

Ahhh, yes, and this transition will give us insight into how we might fit into this complex culture... and I expect it will provide valuable revelations too.

I sat back again and exhaled. Sometimes I asked myself who my Emissary and the rest of our Leadership really were and where they came from. We never saw them, but we put trust in them because we had no alternative. Maybe if we actually got to know them, we would not be as confident in their enlightenment. Their invisibility gave them a kind of invincibility.

The overhead rumble came again. The Emissary continued, *You must be careful, as your friend Ladarius warns you. If you show your Keysian superiority in one great burst, your coach and teammates will begin to suspect that you are separate from them. They will ask questions you will not always be able to answer.*

The Emissary and those above him always seemed to have an innate awareness. They knew if I used my full gamut of Keysian powers, especially my otherworldly speed, that I'd be seen as something other than a Callister Cascades Ram.

I told my Emissary that I liked football. That I thought they had made a wise choice in embedding me in this uniquely American enterprise. But I would go slowly. I'd listen to Ladarius, Coach Sawyer, my teammates, Mr. Fasciola, even Sam the Slam and the electronic game enthusiast. They all had a part to play in how I engaged this new experience.

I loved Keysiana. I knew we might have to abandon it suddenly. I couldn't fail. Our old civilization was under duress, and we might have to relocate to this new one. I was a trailblazer, a harbinger of a new future. If I had to become a Keysian ambassador to American football, I would give it my best effort.

My Emissary entreated: *Sublimious Z. Hormats, a.k.a. Clancy, please become excellent at football, understand it, pass on the intricacies of it to us so that we may fold into the fabric of this great, entangling society if we must.*

And, don't forget, have some fun!

5

Every day was a new learning experience. I tried not to act
like a total novice, but I was when it came to traditions that all other Callister
Cascades players and students took for granted. Before the first game, they had
what they called a "pep rally" in a big auditorium. The school superintendent
proclaimed his pride in unveiling the eighty-third edition of the football Rams.
He was also proud that Alphonse Sawyer was just the eighth head coach in the
school's history.

The student body gave a loud cheer. Our team pumped fists. I shouted,
"Coach is a leader of great sagacity!" Several players on the stage where we all had
gathered peered uncomprehendingly at me. Luckily, my salute was swallowed up
in the supportive noise of hundreds of others.

Coach Sawyer introduced each player, and all stood and waved or made the
"V" for victory sign. When it came to me, he announced that I was the Rams'
new secret weapon. "Soo-blimm-ious Clancy, faster than a speeding bullet."

Many of the team behind me chanted, "Who's he! Who's he!"

I believe they were having some fun at my expense. At least that's what
Ladarius told me. It was sort of a rookie initiation, he said.

On the night of the game, I was impressed by all the organized pageantry that
surrounded the actual playing—the marching band, the cheerleaders, the flag
twirlers, a live ram with its horns painted gold running across the field surrounded by a half-dozen handlers, students and parents in the stands with whistles and

bells and plastic ram horns emitting primitive bleats.

We Keysians had studied these football rituals from a distance. But now I was right in the eye of the storm.

Our quarterback, Prince, slammed my shoulder pads with his fists. "Are you ready, Submarine?!" Teammates were already turning Sublimious into different nicknames.

"I am ready to discover the taste of ultimate victory!"

"I knew you'd be pumped!" Prince shouted back. "Power on!"

We were playing some school from far away. Cathedral Prep came on buses and brought with them carloads of enthusiastic fans. The Prep, as they called themselves, was said to schedule Callister Cascades for their first game because they thought it would be an easy win.

Coach Sawyer gathered the team around him in the center of the field.

"Men," he barked, "you know they whipped us bad last year. But we ain't the same dead possum we were then. We got some weapons, some game-breakers, angry pay-backers. We're gonna show the Preppies we're the new sun rising and we're gonna singe their arrogant asses."

Ladarius leaned over to me and whispered, "Coach can string together some original mental images, can't he?"

I was surprised by the degree of violence in the actual game. In our scrimmages, we collided, but without the bone-jarring impact you could now hear and feel on each play. Coach was using all of us pass-catchers—Aurelius, Styles, Kadeem, Heath, Ladarius and me—to keep us fresh. Prince was hitting us with quick down-and-outs, slants across the middle, screens behind pulling linemen. Running back Junius Jones was gouging the Prepsters with five- and eight-yard bursts.

I felt as if I was fitting into the schemes the coaches had drawn up. I was not being asked to be some lightning streak, blinding dazzled defenders. I ran the short and intermediate routes with my fellow pass-catchers, and Prince drilled us with precise spirals that kept the chains moving.

Once I rocketed ten yards and did a full spin, followed by a backflip. My defender kneed me in my groin pads as I landed. Ladarius swept by and waggled a finger. "Rules of the road, my man!" he admonished.

I acknowledged his reminder and stayed within the game's confines.

Callister Cascades pulled off a huge opening-night upset. Many of us were carried off the field by screaming, jubilant followers. Ladarius's dad, Big Nico, wrapped him and me in his arms. *"Arete!"* he saluted, which I learned meant excellence in Greek. "Maybe we got a killer team at last!"

Coach Sawyer found me in the crush of celebrating fans. "This just the start, Soo—sluv-ius! You came to us outta some dormant volcano or something... and one of these games we're gonna explode you outta the crater summit. Just you wait!"

It felt good to ride the wave of so many elated fans and teammates. I couldn't wait to get back and tell my Emissary what initial success felt like. Maybe I could lead the way to a safe eventual touch-down for my people.

After all, that was the ultimate goal of football, right?

* * *

As I settled into my homeroom each morning at Callister Cascades High, I got to know my classmates and teacher better. Even though I went off and attended different classes during the day, I felt most at ease with these early-morning contemporaries who weren't part of the football team.

Big Hair breathlessly told me about his own version of electronic football on PlayStation in the Cascades Game Hall. His actual name was Burke Pennypack. His family was wealthy, someone told me. They paid for a lot of the computers, controllers, headsets, and keyboards that Burke and his fellow gamers used in the school's specially outfitted e-sports space.

Burke didn't act like he was different from anybody else. His blond hair still grew straight up in a spike. He never cut it, so when it reached a certain apex it folded over and began to envelop his head like a fuzzy cloth. He seemed very smart but obsessed. He spoke of player ratings, wear-and-tear, and classic game modes.

"Your players are on a screen. Did you ever see a game with actual players on a real grass field?" I asked him.

He admitted he rarely had. "I heard our Callister Cascades team is far from perfect. I want players I can draft and customize. I am very good at manipulating them to a win with my joystick."

"Come see us," I told him. "Bring some of your gamer friends. We are going to 'shock the world,' so Coach says. At least in our part of the county and state."

"I might give it a try. Problem is I'm allergic to sunlight."

"You're lucky," I said. "We play most of our games on Friday nights."

I convinced another homeroomer, Samantha Schneider, a.k.a. "Sam the Slam," to attend our first game. When we Rams were announced to the crowd at the start, each player could bring his parents, siblings or significant other to the center of the field. I asked Sam if she would walk out with me.

"You're kidding," she gasped. "No guy has ever asked me to go anywhere."

"Well, I'm not any guy," I assured her.

"You sure aren't. You're either unconscious or a freak."

"Believe me," I said. "I'd be honored to have you go with me."

So, Samantha came in a tanned leather Indian skirt with beads and her custom high boots. She bore a blue tattoo on her left bicep. It was in the shape of a clenched fist. She didn't wear any makeup like the other girls. But she did smell very good, like newly shaved wood chips, "from a neighbor's lathe," she said.

My teammates did a double take. "You brought Sam the Slam?"

"Yes, she is a companion who tells me things that nobody else does."

"Like what? How to cold cock a mule?"

"She has acquainted me with the martial arts."

"Yeah, she'll deep-six you with that stuff, man. She's dusted more than one guy who called her a bull dyke."

"I don't plan to call her that since I don't know what a bull dyke is."

"Don't listen to them," Ladarius confided in me. "Nobody's ever given her a chance. You have."

My homeroom teacher, Mr. Fasciola, was also my US history teacher in a class just before lunch. I wrote down virtually everything he said. In Keysiana, tutors had filled me with the story of America, from the War for Independence to the Civil War to the Great Depression. But Mr. Fasciola was so much more detailed and descriptive than my tutors.

He told us about President Kennedy and how he was shot from 265 feet away as he drove in a Texas motorcade. I asked him afterward why anyone would want to kill an American president. He explained there were rogues who thought they could change history with one rash act. John Wilkes Booth thought he could restore the Confederacy by killing America's greatest president.

I constantly wanted to know more from Mr. Fasciola. I'd keep him after class to ask questions, ignoring both his and my need to eat lunch.

"Why don't they encase your—er, our—most important leader in an impenetrable glass vault when they expose them to the public?" I asked.

"Because they are representatives of all the people," he said.

Of course, I couldn't tell him that we never saw our Emissary or Oracles. We didn't even know when they were replaced, died, or even if they were eternal. The flow of Keysiana wisdom was never interrupted. I could never share our ethos with Mr. Fasciola, but I wanted to learn as much as I could from him. I hoped someday he would tell me his version of the history of American football.

6

Callister Cascades won our first three games. Apparently, it had never happened in recent memory. It was the talk of the school, even the community. When we ate at Ladarius's dad's restaurant, townspeople came by our booth and shook our hands and told us to keep it up. Some paid for our gyros and Cokes. One kid even asked for our autographs.

"What's that all about?" I asked Ladarius.

"You sign your name on a piece of paper. Maybe even his arm."

"Should I put a greeting? 'Have a joyous day, Sublimious Clancy.'"

"Sure. Most just want to be touched by our little success so far."

Ladarius said that the vibe around the team was different than in the past. "Our practices, the brotherhood in the locker room, how the coaches treat us," he said. "There's some real positive energy compared to what we've felt before."

I couldn't agree or disagree, never having been exposed to the way football affects so many in the larger proximity. I just sort of basked in the "good feeling" that Ladarius told me I was part of.

"You know that you have something to do with it, don't you?" he said. "Coach hasn't used you the way he can, but he will. You're gonna burn the enemy when nobody's expecting it. You ready?"

"Certainly," I said. But when I thought about it, I really wasn't prepared for going beyond what I had been asked to do so far.

Ladarius was cool, truly in touch with his surroundings and how everything fit together. I was lucky to have him as my primary guide. Yet I was a little wary he'd push me too far to reveal something that I shouldn't.

"Guys on the team ask me about you," he said, leaning forward in the Drakos booth. "They think I'm closest to you, so they figure I know all sorts of stuff about you. But I really don't when it comes right down to the nub."

I took a deep breath. "What... what is it that they ask?"

"All the normal things. Where you're from? Where you live? Do you have a family? You're different, why is that? They want a fuller picture of you."

I had discussed all of this with the Emissary. We had to be ready for questions. The more I penetrated their world, the more I would be asked to reveal mine.

"As long as I'm a member of the team, does it matter who I am?"

"Well, you sorta came out of nowhere. Guys are curious."

"I'm not really supposed to talk about it," I said, lowering my voice. "My parents came to this country on special visas. They have advanced science degrees, and they're in a government program that is classified. I live with my grandfather in a secure place and see them on weekends."

"Sounds like you practically live on your own."

"I can't tell you any more. Subversives might try to undermine my caretaker and family. I can only tell you I catch a bus near the 7-Eleven out on the pike to get to school every day."

Ladarius wasn't one to try to get me to bare my soul. He had an unusual background himself. His dad had met his American mom when she came to Greece as an adviser during a serious national financial crisis. Big Nico ran a small café that she frequented every day. They fell in love, married and returned to America.

"My mom is African American," he once told me. "She grew up in Philadelphia. Her skin is paler than my father's. I still see her every now and then."

"That's the story of America, isn't it?" I said. "People leave their past behind. They become part of the big homogenized blending machine."

"True," laughed Ladarius. "I wish my mom and dad still blended together."

We ate our gyros, spanakopitas and baklavas that Ladarius's dad brought us. He never charged me a cent. He said I was his son's guest, and it was fuel for peak performance. He was a soccer fan who had converted to American football.

"You like the food my dad makes?" asked Ladarius.

"It's very good. Especially when he keeps bringing it."

"You know he's serious about giving us an edge. He bets on games." Ladarius shook his head. "Bets big-time on college and pros. It's not legal to bet on high school football. But you can't stop so-called friendly wagers. If he keeps the food coming, maybe he thinks it'll swing the odds in his favor. Once you're hooked on gambling, you're hooked."

"You know this football is very complicated," I said. "This betting... you mean money? On which team wins? He might bet on you... me?"

Ladarius looked up from his sweet baklava and shook his head. "Sometimes, Sublim, I ask myself where you came from. Like you've never heard of wagering on games? No wonder guys want to know more about you. When you first arrived, you acted like football was some new, strange plaything. That really couldn't have been true 'cause you're so good at it."

"Well, yes." I sat back, relaxed, and composed as I'd been taught. "My progenitors came from a great distance where football was not part of the normal patterns of life. I needed a guide, and you are it. My coach and teammates too. And even my other classmates. I suck football up, like nectar from flowers as a bird would in exchange for pollination."

"Geez," laughed Ladarius. "You say the damnedest stuff."

"Yes, I do. Don't I?"

"All us Rams gotta wonder about you. But maybe we should just chill out. You're here and we should sit back and enjoy your oddness. It's just who *you are*."

I breathed easier. Had I passed the test?

It felt like I had just slipped over the goal line and barely been touched.

* * *

Before football practice each day, before the Friday night games, I was required to attend classes from eight till three thirty. They included English literature, algebra, biology, American history, Spanish, and a couple of electives—astronomy and culinary arts. I had done my due diligence, as the saying goes. The Emissary had our tutors fill me with as much knowledge as they could to give me the skeletal trappings of an active high school student. Beyond the basics, these counselors advised: Keep your mouth shut, look attentive, take assiduous notes, and find other classmates who can get you through the assignments with passing grades.

To tell the truth, I enjoyed my classes. The teachers were scholarly and lively. I sat in the middle of the room and tried to merge with the crowd. But a teacher would occasionally single me out.

"Mr. Clancy, do you think the rise in average global temperatures of almost two degrees Fahrenheit over the last two decades heralds an apocalypse for humanity over the next half century?" Ms. Carpenter, my biology teacher, asked.

"I certainly hope not, ma'am, if we move here, we do not wish to deal with any extraordinary circumstances we have not foreseen," I answered.

"What do you mean by 'if we move here'? Aren't you here already?"

"Yes, certainly," I faltered a moment. "I meant we just moved to Callister Cascades, and we'd like to make it permanent if we can."

Sometimes I had to cover my tracks, even awkwardly.

Another time, our astronomy teacher asked the general class if we thought the asteroid Apophis offered any threat of colliding with Earth in 2029.

I raised my hand instinctively and replied: "We've done our calculations and believe it will pass within 19,794 miles from this planet's surface."

The teacher blinked. "Whose calculations are you referring to?"

"Uh, er—" I stuttered. "Me and some buddies with a Celestron NexStar telescope. We can follow discernible objects in near space."

Mostly, I remained mute and heedful, like I was tuned in to everything being discussed. With Mr. Fasciola, I really wanted to absorb as much as I could about where America had been and where it might be going. I asked questions about wars, Congress, immigration, women's rights and civil rights, and all other rights of those on the periphery of this vast conglomeration of citizenry.

I studied hard for his tests and spent time in the library doing research for special reports I did: "Two Years in the Wilderness with Lewis and Clark," "How Much Influence Frederick Douglass Had on President Abraham Lincoln," and "How the 1960s Changed America."

When I'd corner Mr. Fasciola after class to ask about some fact I couldn't digest, he'd sometimes joke that he wished more of his students wanted to know as much as I did.

"It's just there's so much in America's past and future I need to comprehend," I told him. "And I hear you're a tough grader."

He'd put an arm around me and walk me to the cafeteria. He was not that interested in missing lunch to ensure that I'd get an A or a B in his class.

"You know, Sublimious, I hear you're pretty darn good at football. You just stay interested in your classes, keep your grades up, and your life will stay in balance. That's all you can ask of yourself."

I thanked him for his advice. He was another bulwark that I needed to make my visitation a valuable experience.

7

Saint Jerome was one of our fiercest opponents. I heard that in the previous season, they knocked our quarterback, Prince, out of the game with a concussion in the second quarter. Then they rolled over us by four touchdowns.

"We're a year older, a year wiser, a year stronger, and a year when your coaches have put together a winning strategy," Coach Sawyer told us at practice.

"What a difference a year makes," a Ram mumbled next to me.

Our offensive coordinator took me aside early in the week before our Friday night game. "Sublimious, the *Jeronimos* (that's what everybody called Saint Jerome students) are known for their speed and over-pursuit. So we're going to use you to turn their aggressiveness back on them."

"Uh-huh," I responded. "I'm ready to do my part."

"If it's close late in the game, Prince is going to pitch to Junius Jones on a wide sweep left. We're going to post you in the slot. You'll come back right, take a handoff from Jones, turn the corner, and kick the burners in. The blur you'll leave will jack the whole stadium off the ground."

"Yes, that sounds like a superlative plan," I said, trying to sound like I could envision what the coach had drawn up for me. It was what Ladarius had suggested. I was going to burn the enemy when nobody was expecting it. I had told Lad I was ready, but in the back of my mind I wondered if I was.

We practiced the reverse all week. We tried me faking a block to the left and then coming back for the handoff. We worked on a pitch from Jones. But what clicked best was little or no deception. I would blaze past Junius, wrap two hands around the football, and turn on the turbojets Coach Sawyer liked so much.

I would blaze to glory, Ladarius said when he heard the plan, just like he'd predicted I would when the coaches realized what they had in their toolbox.

The night of the St. Jerome game was damp and misty. It had rained all day, but it had stopped an hour before game time. The field was soggy, and my nerve endings tingled. The stands were packed. Callister Cascades played a tight, hard-fought game. The action swung back and forth under the bright lights.

The offensive coordinator, Coach Sampson, pulled me aside early in the fourth quarter. "How you feeling, big guy?" He stuck his face right next to mine. Sweat was streaming down his cheeks even though he wasn't playing. I was, I'd caught a couple passes, nothing spectacular. But now my time had arrived.

We had the ball on our forty-yard line and were starting to drive. The game was tied. I could feel the heat and determination coming off each Ram. When I entered the game, everyone on offense knew what I was there for.

Prince barked the signals, took the snap, swung around and handed the ball to Jones. Virtually every Jeronimo followed our workhorse running back to the left. I then broke out of the slot, took a clean handoff, and was off to the races down the right sideline. I felt the jets kick in.

"Roll, baby, roll!" I heard Ladarius yell in my wake.

I hit midfield. The forty. The thirty. The twenty.

Then I saw him. Coming straight at me in his muddy purple and white uni-form, helmet lowered at full ramming speed. Its crown hit the football nestled in the left crook of my arm and it flew into the air.

The football hovered up in the lights for what seemed like forever. The Je-ronimo grabbed it and broke into a sprint the other way. I slid on the wet turf, bracing my fall.

He was gone. Gone, gone, GONE!

Geez... I looked into the night sky, beyond the stadium lights. Looked for the Emissary. For any kind of spiritual help that might come swirling down from the heavens.

It was not coming. I lay sprawled out on my side.

"Sublimious, what have you done?" I said to my yielding hands, to my whole pickpocketed body. "You have let all Callister Cascadians down."

"You have let every Keysianan down."

"Let all your people down. They will never let us come now."

I plowed my helmet into the wet, cleated turf and vowed to disappear.

* * *

When I stumbled to the sideline, Coach Sampson, who had drawn up the play, was the first to greet me. He placed his hands squarely on my shoulder pads and looked me straight in the eye. "Speed kills, but moves make the man," he said simply. "Next time we'll work on the moves."

Ladarious found me slumped on the bench. "You took off like a shot. Trouble was you ran in a straight line. When you see objects in the headlights, it's best to avoid them."

We lost. Lost by less than a touchdown. Lost to a team that had killed us the year before. "We got nothing to feel down about," Coach Sawyer told us in the locker room. "We're making progress. I'm proud of the way you all fought."

Teammates came up to me as I slowly dressed. "Don't worry. We got your back. You make us a better team."

Honestly, I was shocked. If I could have dug a hole and crawled into it immediately after my turnover, I would have. Maybe some players wanted to give me a good, swift kick. But most guys were making a point of saying it wasn't the end of the world. They all seemingly knew what it was like to mess up.

Prince sought me out. "We'll run the same play again, and you'll take it to the house. You gotta outrun the bad luck."

I showered, dressed, and walked out into the stadium oval where the lights still glowed. I heard all sorts of comments from students, fans, parents, even St. Jerome loyalists. Some yelled, "You blew it, knucklehead!" Others shouted, "Can't trust a new kid!" A few called, "Why're you even on the team?"

Burke Pennypacker, the e-game player, sidled up next to me and said, "You know, I would've sworn you had it, the road to glory, man. Always someone coming cross-console to bury you. Next time, I'm taking you off the board before someone lays a bombshell zap on you."

I faked a smile. "Geez, I didn't know you were even playing me."

"Yeah, you're catching on, so I put you in my game, but criminey..."

"I won't make the same mistake again, I promise."

"You better not," said Burke. "Otherwise, I'm gonna have to trade you."

Ladarius pulled me into his car, his dad was driving. Big Nico was quiet for a while, then said, "You're lucky I didn't bet the Rams tonight."

Lad exhaled. "Dad, you know high school games are off-limits for betting."

"Just a small wager with Phil, my buddy who went to St. Jerome."

"Your small wagers are never small," said Ladarius. "You can't be putting that kind of pressure on us. Even if you don't tell us ahead of time."

It took a while for their car to exit the parking lot. The local cops were wielding their flashlights like whirling laser beams. "Last year, there were a quarter of these cars," said Mr. Drakos. "Your games are putting fannies in the seats."

He drove us downtown to his restaurant. More cars were there than usual, even though it was approaching ten o'clock.

"Damn, I'm gonna have to give you some lamb souvlaki tonight. Maybe slip you a glass of wine from Santorini. Your games are building my business."

* * *

Next Monday in homeroom, Sam the Slam poked me in the arm. "I was there Friday night. Saw you blow it," she zinged.

"Yes, I was heartily embarrassed," I said. "I'm sorry you had to see it. Sorry everybody in Callister Cascades saw it."

"Look, man," Sam rumbled. "You got nothing to worry about from me. I don't ever go to football games. You got me to go. That's something!"

"Geez, that's outstanding. I'm so glad you went. What did you think?"

"I'm thinking you shouldn't let some geek-neck take the ball from you."

"Oh, I know," I said. "If I could've gotten on the school newscast this morning, I'd have apologized to every last person within hearing range."

"Horse-bleep!" Sam scoffed. "You don't apologize to nobody for nuthin'. You show up here, get on the team, and they trust you to make a big play in the fourth game of the year. I'm sorta impressed how you're carving out a rep."

I liked Samantha Schneider from the start. She told me what she thought, whether I liked it or not. Hardly anybody else in homeroom spoke to her. Her appearance, her attitude scared them. But I didn't know any better.

"Do you know Ladarius Drakos? He's a pass catcher on the team like me?"

"Name sorta rings a bell."

"His dad has a little restaurant downtown. It's Greek, and it's excellent."

"Yeah, I've heard about it."

"Well, next Friday night after the game, will you join me at the Drakos place? I'll buy you a gyro."

"You sure?" blinked Sam. "Nobody wants to be seen any place with me."

"I'm sure," I said. "We're going to win, and I want you to celebrate with me."

* * *

I reported in periodically. The Emissary had scribes who probably gave him weekly, maybe even daily, accounts, but they weren't embedded with the Americans like I was. On the ground, in the trenches. Playing the game of football, learning its complexities, and attempting to see how it affected virtually every man, woman, and child in one typical community.

In a recent game, you committed a costly mistake, my informants tell me.

My Liege's voice never wavered. It never seemed angry or excited, confused or taunting. It awaited feedback so it could fold it into a vast databank that might give Keysiana a better read on its future integration prospects.

"Yes, I was ready for instant vilification, but the response was mixed. I began to react like a typical human and to bury my head in humiliation. Yet I received mainly support from those who know the most about football."

Did you learn anything that might help us?

"Well, I found that those Americans want me to succeed because I will help them succeed. I suspect they will not tolerate many more mistakes as I become adept at their game. They are only so forgiving, but they've extended me a reasonable learning curve."

And the rest of your immediate social structure, your schoolmates who do not play, do they care whether your team succeeds or fails?

"Oh, they care all right. Care to the point of burning your ears off. But they don't have as much at stake, so their facile judgments fade away quickly," I replied.

Would you say the entire community cares, or at least the majority of it? Does their mental health and daily life change, depending on victory or defeat?

I was billeted again in the safe house. I began pacing the floor. "That is a very good question. I have not been here long enough to fully observe many of the Cascadians beyond the school. But they've begun showing up more often than in the past for our games. The town identifies with us when our achievements suffuse it with positive energy. That is what Ladarius and my teammates tell me."

The Emissary seemed to breathe deeply. Since I couldn't see him, I had to listen for near-imperceptible indications of whether I was telling him anything useful. I couldn't tell exactly what he and the Higher Powers truly wanted. As far as I knew, football was only one segment of American civilization and culture that Keysiana had chosen to penetrate.

There were hints that explorers had been sent to blend into and comprehend private enterprise, government, volunteer and religious organizations, various forms of media, and the emotional differences of the sexes. I didn't know any of the others who had been sent or why. But I knew each assignment mattered. The Emissaries and Oracles did not examine these other institutions for the sake of simply accumulating knowledge. They knew something threatened our people, and we had to be ready for a sudden transition.

Where do we go from here? the Emissary asked. *We are only into the first portion of the season. You are merely tapping the surface of how football might help us with any possible assimilation.*

"Frankly, sire, I have kept many of my special skills under wraps. If I just slowly learn and contribute, I might open some avenues for our people to integrate into Callister Cascades and beyond. I'd be honored to partly lay the grounds for a Keysian network in mainstream America."

That's very dedicated. But go slowly. We don't want to raise suspicions that we are anything but what we are.

"I believe I have a very important mission. I'm not about to jeopardize it," I responded.

By the way, the Emissary said with an almost jaunty tone, *what do they think of your name, Sublimious?*

"Oh, they think it's pretty cool. It sets me apart."

Not too far apart, we trust.

"No, sire. I tell the ones who can't handle it to call me Clancy. They think it sounds macho, like I'm one of their kickboxers about to engage in what they call a cage fight."

Yes, it is a strange land and tribe we are scouting. Violence and proving your manhood are like an elixir to them.

8

AFTER SCHOOL, PRACTICES LASTED ONE AND A HALF HOURS, sometimes two. Coach Sawyer was assisted by five other coaches, all Callister Cascades teachers with previous football experience. One coach was like a psychologist. The players called him "Shrink." You could go to him if you had problems—in the classroom, at home, with a girl, with your diet, with other teammates.

Practices were well-organized. We were divided into units: offensive line, running backs, quarterbacks, defensive line, linebackers, corners and safeties. And then there was *us*. Pass-catchers, I called us at first. But Ladarius said we were wide receivers. "The heart and soul of our fast-strike air force," he boasted.

For much of the practices, we worked separately with Prince and two other backup QBs. We ran routes, perfected receiving techniques, did downfield blocking drills, worked on spacing against zone defenses, and learned to break off routes when Prince got in trouble.

Coach Sampson was the coach who spent a lot of time with us. We called him "Tarzan" when joking around. He wore short sleeves even in the coldest weather to show off his muscular arms and chest. He could catch a pass behind his back, flip the football up over his head and nestle it in his hands in front of him. (I didn't tell anybody, but I could do the same thing my first day on the field.)

After time together, the receivers became a tight fraternity. Most were black or at least dark-skinned. Except for our pale 6-foot-4 tight end, Heath, and me. My skin tone was close to what might be called golden. When I sweat, my epidermis glistens like it's polished. Aurelius, Styles and Kadeem couldn't get over this.

"What are you, man, some kind of surfin' Polynesian?"

"No, no," Styles would say. "He was raised in the desert and chased greyhounds. That's why he's so damn fast."

"Hey, I'm sayin' he's black like us," said Kadeem. "He ducks into a spray-paint booth in the locker room before he come out on the field like a gold Superman."

Ladarius knew a little more than the others did. He knew what I had told him about my parents coming here under special visas and working for the government, and me living with my grandfather and only seeing them on weekends. Still, I didn't tell him where I came from or how my skin got so gold-leafed. I wasn't like any color or ethnicity he or his teammates had seen.

Black athletes were faster than whites, we all knew. I, however, the golden Sublimious, was seconds faster than any of them. My pass-catching teammates couldn't compute that dichotomy. They swore some experimental doctor had implanted an extra pair of speed ligaments in my thighs or knees. Or as Coach Sawyer swore: I was outfitted with turbojets from an F-15 striker jet.

I just kept the secret of my speed to myself. I remained humble, didn't boast or preen. I always heard Ladarius's warnings in the back of my mind: "Stay within the confines of the game" and "Remember the rules of the road." I told the other receivers that I watched and learned from them, and they made me an honorary brother.

"You got the speed, Sublim, but you don't got the moves yet. You don't got the jukes, the rub-offs, the nudges, the one-handers, the hip waxers, the sideline toe-taps, the ref cheats . . ."

"We can teach you all that," said Aurelius. "But that might mean you steal playin' time from us, and we gotta protect our self-interests."

* * *

The Rams' next opponent was Howell Tech. My teammates respected the *Howlin' Hounds.* They said the school combined academics with occupational prep like auto repair, welding and electronics. Its students were smart and disciplined, and its team played not for college scholarships but for pride and each other.

"Men, they'll throw complicated defenses and motion offenses at us 'cause their coaches know they got guys who like puzzle-solving," Coach Sawyer told us.

He took me aside again and said he was going to give me another shot at kick and punt returns. He assigned Demon Dan Kerkegaard to bring me up to speed. Coach Sawyer leaned into me with his rumpled cap almost touching my nose. "We know you got the jets. Now you just summon the brains which, we're sure you got too," he said confidently. Coach was always trying to instill something undefinable in me, which he couldn't exactly define.

Demon Dan knew I had the hands and the vision to field footballs kicked high in the air and arcing down toward my tall, wiry frame. The secret, he said with his dented face, was to get in the flow behind the blocking wedge on kickoffs and to read that one key block on punts and then press "the pedal to the metal."

We tried it over and over in practice, and he kept yelling, "NO, NO, NO! WATCH ME!"

Demon Dan was compact, obsessive. He'd catch a kick, fuse in behind five large blockers, and come out the other end like a human torpedo. We practiced over and over until all of us on the Rams' special teams were sick and dizzy from the monotony.

The Thursday before the Howell Tech Friday night game, Demon Dan declared we finally had it. "Especially you, Clancy. You seem like you have a built-in computer which allows you to calculate your 'escapability threshold,' and when you see the tunnel open, you take off."

He didn't know how right he was.

That cool, crisp night, the ball came soaring out of the lights, and my brain—

in one one thousandth of a nanosecond—signaled this was the purest of chances. I caught the punt, juked right like my brothers had taught me, caught a seam through the swarm of Howlin' Hounds, and blasted into the ionosphere. I never looked back.

I sprinted through the endzone, curled around one corner, and jogged back to Demon Dan and handed him the ball. Ladarius, I'm sure, loved my deferential genuflection to the rules of the road. We won the game by five points, just as we had lost the game the week before by a slim margin through my miscue.

Coach said I was coming along nicely for "an unknowable receptacle."

* * *

After the game, I found Samantha Schneider under the stands. She said she didn't want to wait out on the track surrounding the field because she was self-conscious. I knew this wasn't true. Maybe she just didn't want to be seen at a school function.

We loaded into Ladarius's dad's car. Big Nico had a wide smile on his face. Maybe he had placed a bet on our game, against his son's wishes, and won.

The night had been cold, and Sam was wearing jeans, boots and a big parka with a fur collar. She said it was wolf. Ladarius told her it had better not be, since they were an endangered species. I think sometimes Sam the Slam just liked to pretend to be a rebel.

In his restaurant, Big Nico looked at Sam sideways. She had arranged her hair into a frizzy blonde bowl and had a stick-on (at least I think it wasn't permanent) tattoo of a guillotine on her cheek. Her shirt was tanned leather with pocket fringe.

Lad told his dad, "Sam likes to shock people. Sublim lets her hang around with him because he doesn't know any better."

We both laughed. I liked Sam because she was natural and outspoken. I was her only ally in homeroom, and Ladarius was right: I didn't know any better, and I didn't care that the others froze her out. She told me the ones who called me "a loser" after I fumbled away our first loss. And she would identify the same ones who'd come to congratulate me now for being a "hero."

I didn't grasp that word, *hero*. And I don't think Sam liked it much. The designation could come and go depending on your most recent performance.

"Sublim's never returned punts before this week," explained Ladarius.

"Well, as far as I can see," said Sam. "You just have to catch a ball sailing out of the sky and then outrun everybody."

"Yeah, that's pretty much it, but you see, he didn't have any idea he could do it until the instant he did it."

"Isn't that called genius?" Sam grinned.

"No, no, no," I protested. "I don't like that word either. I'm not special. I don't want anybody on the team or in our school to think it."

"You better watch it," Sam said. "Weenies will be talking about you on Tik-Tok, or some influencer will do a podcast on Spotify and tell all sorts of lies about you."

I looked at her like I knew what she was referring to, but I didn't. I was aware that a lot of my classmates' lives centered around texting and using Facebook on their cell phones. But my Keysian tutors had only provided a cursory overview of this communications phenomenon. I'd have to rely on friends like Sam and Ladarius to acquaint me with all its interpersonal nuances.

Big Nico brought out a large covered dish and set it in the middle of the table. It contained the Greek dish moussaka made of eggplant and ground lamb in a thick béchamel sauce, layered in a light toasted crust. He cut us pieces with a knife he called a *kopis*.

"Gawd, do you eat here a lot?" Sam asked me.

"After practice sometimes, and every night we have a game."

"Why the blazes aren't you bigger than you are?"

"I have a high metabolism. It takes a lot to rev my engine."

Big Nico sat down with us. "You know, townies are starting to love this team. I'll keep you stocked with food if you keep on rolling like you are."

Even though it was late, around eleven o'clock, the interior of the Drakos restaurant was festive. Cascadians had come to eat and celebrate. Some stopped by our booth to tell us we had given their burg a new spirit and prestige. "We've never beat Great Grantham before. Now we got a chance," they'd tell Ladarius and me with buoyant voices about an upcoming game.

"Don't know if that 'great' is with a small *g* or a cap," laughed Big Nico.

Samantha Schneider was eating her moussaka with as much gusto as I was. No one would think her svelte. She could pack it in. I wondered if Nico would consider her part of our "crew" and not charge her for her healthy portions.

"If you want," Sam suddenly said to me, "I could monitor your traffic on social media if you'd like. You know, see if they say good or bad stuff about you."

"Does it matter? I don't have a phone, so I am unaware."

"Oh, I don't doubt that," she smiled mischievously.

"I'd leave Sublim in the dark," laughed Ladarius. "He's better off."

Mister Drakos nodded and gave me another helping of moussaka. "You don't know how many customers come in here and stare at their phones through a meal."

I looked around the booth and thought, *I'm glad to have such friends. They will take care of extraneous things so I can do what I must in my assignment.*

PART TWO

Recognition

9

When the weather grew colder, football gained momentum in the greater American landscape. Schools had parades and bonfires and rallies where even people who had no interest in the actual games came to sing, cheer, laugh, and drink everything from hard cider to beer out of giant steins. Whole teams walked down the center of towns, as mayors gave them keys to the city and bystanders threw confetti at them.

This was all new to me, of course. As with everything else associated with football, Ladarius was my mentor. He told me that Callister Cascades was like most other small to medium towns in the United States. It had its traditions, whether it was winning or losing, and whether its citizens cared or just went through the motions.

The present year was sort of astonishing, he said. Townies came up to him and asked, "You play for the Rams? We're glad you've finally given us some hope."

We had three wins against the agonizing loss to St. Jerome. When we played an away game against Greys Ferry, we "fumble-fucked" around for three quarters, so said Coach Sawyer. Then he called an amazing play to shake us out of our lethargy. He had Prince drop back deeper than usual and toss a screen left to Ladarius, who started to run behind a wall of blockers. Suddenly he stood straight up and chucked a long overhand lateral to me on the other side of the field.

Greys Ferry was stunned. The pass hit me in the numbers, and I turned on the turbojets, scoring the game-changing touchdown.

I couldn't believe how many Cascadians swarmed the field at the final gun and embraced us, me in particular. It had been Coach, I tried to tell them. He had turned the tide. And Ladarius had thrown the perfect pass almost fifty yards. But I guess I was the most visible recipient of this clever deception, so they pounded my shoulders, squeezed my chest, and kissed my cheeks—females mostly.

At school, I was inundated by people I'd never seen before. On social media, Sam said I was the subject of posts and threads, friendings and likes, and Instagram and YouTube videos of my game-winning score.

"You don't know any of that, do you?" laughed Sam. "Actually, who really cares? Unknown sources trash me all the time, when they even think of me."

"I guess I probably should follow what's going on," I responded.

"Hey, you got people talking, even if they ghost you. You let me screen your posts and tweets while you concentrate on the important stuff."

"That would be wondrous. When they come up to me, I could tell them that Samantha Schneider is handling all my extraneous matters."

Sam wrinkled her brow. "Nah, I wouldn't do that. Don't ever mention me. You just smile, play football, and blow other teams away."

"I'll get a phone and put my name in it," I said. "I'll give it to you, and every now and then, you give me a report on what people are saying."

"Put your jersey number on it: 'Clancy-15.' It'll give 'em something to shoot their wad over. Tell you how great you are or how you can be even greater."

I loved that tattooed fist on Sam's arm. It said everything about her.

*   *   *

We played three more games at the end of October and into November. My teammates said we were on a roll. In the first game, I returned a kickoff 100 yards. I'd never had more fun in my life winding through big clumps of bodies and spinning out of the grasp of two tacklers who cursed when I sprang free. The last man between me and the goal line tried to punch the ball out of my hands. Instead, I drove the cowhide into his face mask, and he fell over backward.

I wasn't usually that hostile. But my wide receiver teammates gave me high-fives and told me I was learning to be mean, MEAN. *Mother-f—-ing MEAN!*

In the next game, I caught two touchdown passes when I accelerated past my defenders, and Prince laid soft thirty-yard passes in my hands. He told me on the sidelines, "You're making it easy, Sublim. I just have to wind up and throw the ball as far as I can, and you'll run under it."

That night after the game, I was invited to a party at Burke Pennypack's house. He was the classmate who ran the e-sports venue at school. He lived in a mansion and must have invited half of Callister Cascades High. An actual band was playing in the living room. People were dancing, drinking and smoking earthy-smelling cigarettes. One girl even asked me if I wanted to go upstairs to a bedroom.

"Is that a good idea?" I said to her. "What if Burke's parents are up there trying to sleep?"

She smiled at me. "Do you hear the noise level in this place?"

Well after midnight, Burke stopped the band and assembled many of the football team in the center of the living room. "Hey, these guys are the reason we can raise some merry hell," he hooted. "Ten Cent and Electronic Arts are gonna have to make whole new e-games featuring them."

He held a giant goblet with both hands and passed it around so each of us could take a drink. The liquid tasted like it might lift the back of my head off.

Burke wrapped his arms around me and shouted, "Yo, all of you, we got a special player here in Sublimious Clancy! He materialized out of nowhere, and I'm already putting him in my e-games. Let's give him a big thank you for igniting our football season."

Everybody started cheering, and my teammates began pushing me back and forth. It almost felt like they were trying to hurt me. I gave Ladarius a questioning look when I got to him.

"Geez, cool it, Sublim," he hollered. "It's a sign we love you."

During the third game, Coach Sawyer came up to me late in the third quarter with spittle flecking his lips. "Jesus, Soo-bloom-ius, you gotta do something to break this game open!"

I knew he wasn't really leaving it solely in my hands. He called for a flea flicker. Prince handed the ball to Junius Jones as if it were a dive into the line. Then suddenly he turned and pitched it to Prince behind him. I ran a "go" route straight down the center and got open by twenty yards. However, the pass wasn't one of Prince's finest. I had to stretch with all my substantial length and reel the ball in with my fingertips. As I tightened my grip, I did a full frontal flip to maintain possession as I cleared the goal line. I knew Ladarius would not be happy.

"No showboatin'!" I imagined him yelling in my ears.

Instead, I was crushed by my teammates in the endzone. "My gawd!" shouted Styles, "You killed that invert more than any of us brothas could've."

I went with Ladarius and Sam afterward to the Drakos restaurant. We were getting to be a regular crew. Lad and his dad were acclimating to Sam the Slam's eccentricity. She had invited some young guy, maybe he was from our high school, to interview me for his podcast.

He sat in the booth and thrust a microphone across the table. "Where has Callister Cascades been hiding you for the past couple of years?" he asked.

"I'm new to the team," I answered. "New to football, really."

"You're kidding? You're hearing this right here on the *Josh Higby Show* for the first time," he said to his unseen audience.

"Well, if you never played before," Josh stammered, "how'd you become like, er, this phenom so fast? I mean, you're helping change Cascades' fortunes."

"Oh, it's friends like the fellow sitting next to us, Ladarius Drakos." I nodded across the booth. "He clued me into the intricacies of the game."

"Yes, and we're eating in the Drakos restaurant in downtown Callister Cascades," Ladarius blurted into the mic. "Come here after every game."

"Is that the key?" smiled the podcaster. "Food smells delicious."

I was coming out of my shell, Sam added to the livestream. "Our school and the town are starting to recognize Sublimious. Don't know if he can handle it." She turned to me and asked, "How's it feel to become a celebrity?"

"I'm not sure. I didn't come here to be anything other than a football player. Can any of you tell me how I should feel?" I asked the whole table.

The podcaster said, "Man, if it was me, I'd bask in the whole bright spotlight."

Ladarius leaned back against the booth's cushions. "Spotlights are not really Sublim's thing. He doesn't care much for all the hallelujahs. He probably wouldn't mind chucking all that excess out the window."

The podcaster spoke directly into the mic. "You hear that, all you listeners out there. We've got an emerging star who isn't striving to become a commander of the universe. Do you think that's possible in this day and age?"

Sam laughed. "Our podcast host suddenly wants to stir up a controversy."

"I don't know," said the podcaster. "I think it's sort of refreshing. This young man is so modest he actually appears to want to remain anonymous."

I kept my mouth shut. I knew that's what Ladarius would have counseled. My Emissary and Oracles, too. Football was my reason for being. At least in my present state. Perhaps my Masters might choose a different path for me in the future. As for now, I was paving the way for the larger Keysian community.

Things, though, were getting more complicated. I anticipated they would.

* * *

Mr. Fasciola suggested we eat lunch together after his history class. I brought two roast beef and cheese subs for us from the 7-Eleven where I caught the bus in the morning. We sat at two desks in his homeroom and stretched out our legs.

He said he'd been to a couple of our school's games recently and been impressed, especially with my performance. "I've always been curious about top performers. What do they know of the game? Do they study its history?"

"Sooo…" I hesitated. "Is this a test?"

"No, no. I simply thought that since you're always so inquisitive about American history, do you know the evolution of the game you're so good at?"

My antennae went up. "Should I?" My tutors had acquainted me with some football milestones, but their review was cursory and limited.

"Yes, as a teacher, I think it matters."

I scoured my mind. "Well, I know the first game was played more than 150 years ago. It was nothing like the game we play today."

"That's right, it was just a giant scrum. Then, a player named Walter Camp started to lay out some rules. That sort of mirrors how our society develops. It's a wild free-for-all, and then we impose standards so there's more uniformity."

"Like our refs. Seems to be a lot of them on the field and they blow their whistles at the darnedest times." I didn't want to say too much to demonstrate how much of an apprentice I still tended to be.

"Football has always been violent and dangerous," Mr. Fasciola continued. "It's why it appeals to us. We are unapologetic about our love for its brute-force savagery. But back in 1905, President Theodore Roosevelt threatened to abolish the game because nineteen players had died in collisions and pileups. It seems somebody in our society always steps in to restore order. College presidents were forced to regulate the game or see it die."

"Yeah, but fortunately, they didn't take out all the collisions."

"You're right. We still have them because fans and players feed on them. The public still has a voice."

Mr. Fasciola seemed to have a list. "Another thing: There's constant change and innovation, which matches the growth of our nation. First, they set rules for first downs, then came the forward pass, blocking and three-point stances, single wings, double reverses, and zone defenses. Great coaches from Pop Warner, Knute Rockne, and Bear Bryant to Paul Brown, Tom Landry, and Bill Walsh always added some new wrinkle nobody had ever thought of before."

"Similar to our coaches, Sawyer, Sampson and Demon Dan."

Mr. Fasciola chuckled. "I wouldn't quite put them in the same pantheon, but they're not doing a bad job this year."

I always liked Mr. Fasciola's combination of seriousness and wit. Every so often in class, he'd ask all of us at that very moment whether we were thinking of the First Amendment to the Constitution or who we might be going out with that weekend. It would always snap us out of our daydreaming.

When we were halfway through our subs, he asked, "What do you think makes football go round in this country? What's at the heart of it all?"

I wasn't sure. I'd only been playing for two months. I blurted, "How a win or a loss makes everyone feel each week?"

"No, I'm not thinking of the parochial. I'm referring to what makes it so pervasive to so many in America for at least half the year."

"Geez, as I said, I'm new here in Cascades..."

"Well, I'd say, like so much else, it centers around money. The good ol' American buck. You know, the first radio broadcast of a game was in 1921. Then a sportswriter, Grantland Rice, wrote about Notre Dame's Four Horsemen. TV came along and began telecasting games. Now there are games on every minute of every weekend, and pro football would put a game on at two o'clock in the morning if it could. And it's all to sell beer and cars and deodorant, and the big-name players are better known than our presidents and a few make close to half a billion dollars."

Mr. Fasciola caught his breath and ate the rest of his sub.

"I'll think about all this," I finally said to my teacher. "When I leave the huddle and line up to run my pass route, I'll hear you in my head telling me about the evolution of the game I'm playing."

Mr. Fasciola began to laugh so that his large body and manicured beard began to shake. "One thing to consider, Sublimious," he said as his mirth ebbed. "Look around you out there on that field. You are surrounded by the true definition of American meritocracy. Most of your fellow receivers are black. I don't know what you are, but you and they are there because you're the best."

"I'm golden," I noted. "My speed is providential, so says Coach Sawyer."

"Football's come a long way. Of Division I college players, almost 50 percent are black. In pro football, the ratio is 75 percent black. But they can be Samoan or Australian or Nigerian or German. Players come from all levels of our society. If you're as good as the next guy, you'll get a shot."

I shared my Tastykake dessert with Mr. Fasciola.

"That is very good to hear," I said. "I've been told that American football is fair. At least on the field. There are other parts that I have yet to get used to, but I try to apply myself. It is very important that I learn as much as I can. We'll have to have lunch again, so we can share more of our food and our findings."

10

Callister Cascades was to play its big game against Great Grantham on Thanksgiving Day. The showdown everyone had been waiting for. I learned the school wasn't Great Grantham. It was actually *Greater* Grantham—a school district that consolidated three towns and environs. So, it had many more players to draw from than we did.

Coach Sawyer told our team that Grantham had "owned" us the last several years. "No more," he declared. "This is the year we reap fiery retribution and dismal consequences upon them."

Ladarius said that, it being Thanksgiving, it was Coach's fire-and-brimstone pilgrim preacher speech.

I, of course, had to study the reason for the American holiday. My tutors had been sort of hazy about foreigners—Europeans from England and Holland?—settling in a vast wilderness on the other side of the Atlantic Ocean, and the Indians being ambivalent about their arrival. But the Pilgrims had survived, so their ancestors set aside a special day of gratitude to their deity each year.

Still, it was hard to compute marching parades with Snoopy balloons and large family gatherings gorging on turkey and piles of food with a football game in between.

"We're gonna crack heads," teammate Aurelius vowed, "in front of a raw-throat crowd ready to celebrate some big-time ballin'."

Nevertheless, with such diverse happenings going on, I was primed. The

Cascades coaches told me in the two weeks we had to prepare for the game that they were going to entrust me with an important new assignment.

Greater Grantham had the best and fastest wide receiver we would face all year, Jeopheus "The Burner" Bormelo. He'd already caught twelve touchdown passes of more than twenty-five yards. Rumor had it that he boasted that no defensive back could even come close to covering him. He was headed to Louisiana State University as a way station to greatness in the NFL.

Demon Dan Kerkegaard was going to instill in me the techniques to stop the Burner and lead us to our biggest victory in years. In addition to being a receiver and a return specialist, I was now to become a "shut-down" defensive corner.

"Whew, man," said Ladarius, "you're becoming our Swiss Army knife."

I didn't know what that meant, but my other teammates were saying the coaches were piling a lot on my plate. I knew it wasn't turkey and all the fixings. Since I was fast and smart, they figured I had the best chance of covering the Burner.

Demon Dan worked with me separately from the rest of the team. He showed me how to react to a wide receiver's rhythm, how to bump and run, and force the Burner to the sidelines to cut down on his options. "Keep your eyes on his number so when he leaps, you leap. Watch for a foot plant, which will tell you he's running a stop-and-go."

Dan was relentless. He made me come at first light, before school. He showed me film of Burner and isolated certain frames to pinpoint how he positioned himself or used his hands to get separation.

"Sometimes you step on the tops of his shoes, accidentally, of course."

At first, I was wary. This Burner had the capacity to burn me to the ground.

Coach Sawyer came up to me the day before the game. "Look, Sub-boom-lius, don't know how you got here, but you're the gift that keeps on giving. We got so much con-fiii-dence in you, we're gonna stick you out on an island with their best."

Sometimes I had to ask Ladarius what Coach was telling me. "He means he trusts you more than his own play-calling."

On the day of the game, a parachutist jumped right into the middle of the field and delivered the football to the refs. I thought that was a route I could suggest to the Emissary to deliver the Keysians when it might become necessary.

As play began, Bormelo caught a pass on me over the middle for about thirty yards. "Looks like it's gonna be a piece of cake today, with you covering me," he sneered in my face.

"That is the last one you catch for a long, long time," I countered.

He couldn't believe I would be that cocky.

The next pass, I knocked the ball out of his grip. Then I leaped over him to tip a pass away. I stayed with him on a long route, and a pass hit the back of my helmet.

"Hey, joker, get your funky ass outta the way," he growled.

When Grantham tried a long rainbow down the middle and Burner thought he had his big breakthrough catch, I nudged him at the last second and knocked the ball into the air. I then intercepted it and took it back sixty-eight yards for a touchdown.

The Callister Cascades' stands went wild, and Demon Dan gave me a bear hug.

In the second half, Burner Bormelo couldn't solve me any better. I knocked him off his route once, and he kneed me in the groin. Another pass went right through his hands because I was screening him. Finally, in the last quarter, I matched him step for step on a deep route and stole a pass right out of his hands. Burner took off his helmet and threw it at me. I suggested to him that his action was "rather unsportsmanlike."

He was ejected from the game. We won, 30-17.

Cascadians buried us beneath a huge "dogpile" at the center of the field. I'd never heard of such an enthusiastic enterprise. I was at the bottom of the human pyramid. Luckily, Samantha Schneider dug through the mass with her tattooed, muscular arms and rescued me.

"Ja-zooz, don't you have enough sense to avoid a heap of bodies?"

"I am not aware that people celebrate in such a fashion," I replied.

Ladarius and his dad pulled Sam and me into the car and drove to the Drakos restaurant.

"You guys," cheered Big Nico, "are in the district and state playoffs. I just might have to place a small wager on you."

Lad stared at him angrily. We were still wearing our dirty uniforms.

Diners came up and gave me high-fives. "You shut down their hot-shit, big-time receiver. How'd you do it?" they asked, amazed.

I was somewhat startled. I didn't expect such accolades. Sam said she was fielding all the posts on my social media platform. "Whoa, Sublimious, most want to celebrate by doing all sorts of pleasurable things to you. Most are obscene."

Was I on the verge of taking my game—and life—to a whole new level?

* * *

The Monday following the Grantham victory on Thanksgiving, I was invited to be interviewed in the school's high-tech audio room. The transmission was to go out to all classrooms during homeroom period before the main classes began. I tried to get out of such a public appearance, arguing that Prince or Ladarius or Coach Sawyer or even our behemoth middle guard, Stewey Shavers, would be a more appropriate guest.

"We want you," said the emcee. "You put the clamps on Burner Bormelo, one of the best offensive players in the state. Everyone wants to hear how you and the team did it."

By chance, gamer Burke Pennypack was the emcee.

I sat across from Burke with a mobile microphone in front of me. He had a black headset on like some professional newscaster. "This is going out to the entire school during first homeroom. Everybody's still celebrating our mind-blowing win."

"My goodness," I said into the mic, "I didn't realize how much it mattered. We are all glad, the whole team, I mean, to contribute to such a marvelous feeling of well-being throughout Callister Cascades."

"Well, how'd you do it?" asked Burke, groping for the words. "Grantham's been great, bashing us for years, and now we knock them off with room to spare. It's gotta be the upset of the year."

"It was a team win. We played together. Everybody did their job. I followed a brilliant game plan drawn up by our coaches to stop the Burner."

I had heard all these clichés previously. I think Ladarius had filled my head with them. I could not forget his straight-and-narrow admonitions.

"I have to wonder, though," said Burke, "this is your first year playing with the Rams. How were we so lucky to get someone as good as you?"

My eyes widened. I could answer in generalities, but Burke was probing a little too close to home.

"Well, all I had to do was transfer into this school district. It made me eligible to play football like any other student."

"We didn't have to recruit you or anything?" Burke asked with a chuckle. "I didn't have to promise to put you in one of our e-sports leagues?"

"Nope, first day I came out, they gave me a uniform."

"Simple as that. You never played anywhere else? Never played in Texas or Florida or one of those football hotbeds?"

"No, no, I've always enjoyed watching the game. I figured I'd give it a try on the first day I got here. And the coaches, they just coached me up."

I wanted to give Burke Pennypack a hip bump. *Hey, friend, I don't want to talk about me. It would give me pleasure to discuss the team, our victory, and how the coaches honed my skills to help us win. But don't make it about me.* Such answers might reveal too much, and then I would betray my people and my mission.

"Another thing," said Burke. "How'd you get that name, Sublimious?"

I hesitated. "It is my God-given name. My parents must have thought it suited their child."

"And your parents, where are they from? Are they from another country?"

"Don't forget my last name is Clancy. That's American, isn't it?"

"Yes, I suppose," said Burke.

I hoped that I had cunningly deflected him off such a revealing line of questioning. I silently mouthed across to him, "Keep it on football."

"Sooo, Sublimious Clancy, you've been here three months. What's our team's next goal? Do you think we could possibly go anywhere in the playoffs?"

"I think the sky's the limit. We are just hitting our stride, and we've got as good a chance as anybody." I tried to remember what Ladarius might tell me to say, copying some harmless babble our coaches would trot out.

"In other words, you're not sayin', you'll just be playin'." Burke leaned back, smiling in his headphones as if he had coined something very clever.

"Well, thank you very much, Sublimious Clancy. You and the Rams go do something that will make all of us proud." He signed off with a thumbs up.

When I returned to homeroom, Samantha Schneider nudged me and said, "You sounded like a real dork on the PA interview. Couldn't you have said something a little more original? Like, we're going to cream our next opponent?"

"I don't even know who our next opponent is."

"That doesn't matter. Superman always defeats Lex Luthor." Sam smiled. "You've got a few things to learn, boy. I can be a tough teacher."

11

A stranger showed up at practice asking for me. Coach Sawyer said I had five minutes to speak with him. "He's some college bird dog. I don't want him disturbing your concentration on our upcoming playoff."

The man was waiting at an endzone entrance. He wore what I think they called a safari hat, a rumpled jacket, and khakis.

"Gene Pelfry, regional scout, MAC conference." He vigorously shook my hand.

"Your coach gave me five minutes. Is he a hard ass or what?"

"Coach Sawyer is eminently organized."

"Yes, well, MAC stands for Mid-American Conference. Twelve medium-sized midwestern colleges and members of the Football Bowl Subdivision—schools like Miami of Ohio, Ohio University, Toledo, Bowling Green, Central and Eastern Michigan. We play good competitive football and send our share of boys to the pros."

Mr. Pelfry unveiled a map of the school locations on his laptop.

"Now, Mr. Clancy, you showed up on our radar because of your multifaceted performances. Wide receiver, punt returner, secondary defender. We requested film from your school. What we saw impressed the heck out of us."

I was maybe a head taller than Mr. Pelfry. His shoulders were about three times wider. He resembled one of our offensive guards, only fifteen years older.

"We've zeroed in on your 40-dash time. Three-point-nine seconds...is that a misprint, Mr. Clancy?"

"No, that's what my friend Ladarius timed me. Coaches did too."

"Guess it's not a fluke then. That's what our timers are saying, too. Faster than spit flying in a windstorm."

"Well, sir, I would think it would be very difficult to clock spit."

"Listen, I don't got much time here," said Mr. Pelfry. "Our schools wanted to get in on the ground floor. There'll be other colleges and conferences coming after you with your kinda knock-out speed, but this is your first year playing, right?"

"Yes, I just came out for the Callister Cascades High team this year."

"So, you're a project in the making. Just starting to get the lay of the land."

"Sir, I do know the rules of the road."

The man smiled at me a little crookedly. "Just think about this, will you, please? Consider the MAC schools as a launching pad. You're young and learning, and our college football programs can be a foundation. Then, if you want to use the transfer portal, you can go anywhere your talent may take you. Or if you're comfortable with one of our campuses, you can stay there and the pros will, sure as the day is long, find you and you'll get your pay day."

"My pay day? Sir, I can honestly say I have not been thinking of that at all."

"Of course not," said Mr. Pelfry. "You're bending the curve, and you don't quite know how far it can reach. You're just playing ball 'cause you're hell on wheels and you're having a great time with your buddies dropping the hammer on teams that don't know what's hit 'em."

The man took a card from the brim of his hat and handed it to me. "You got questions, don't hesitate to call. I'll tell you about any of our MAC schools. I'll put you in touch with their head coaches. They're always looking for unformed clay they can work with and turn into a Picasso."

I went back to practice. Coach Sawyer called over to me, "Guy blow smoke up your ass, Sly-boom-lius? Not worth listening till you've hung some pelts on the wall. Then you'll have to beat 'em off with an oar paddle."

* * *

The high school football playoffs were something else I had to learn. If your team won its conference, it qualified. The state was divided into four geographical regions. We were in the Southeast. Four schools qualified in each region, so there were two games on the first weekend. Callister Cascades was matched with New Cambria. The only thing our coaches told us was that historically they were good, and this year their quarterback, nicknamed "The Rifle," was headed for Penn State.

"We're running into all these guys with fancy-dan monikers," said Coach. "It gives us incentive to shuffle them back to when they were nothing-burgers."

Ladarius agreed. "We can chop another big-timer down to size."

Naturally, I didn't know much about our team's past. But enough people like Burke Pennypack and Ladarius's dad and even Mr. Fasciola filled me in. We were perpetual underachievers, never big enough to field consistently strong teams and never so small as to be called "giant killers."

Other teams in the playoffs didn't know what to make of us. We had come out of nowhere. Prince had matured as a seasoned quarterback who made good decisions and could throw short or deep. Running back Junius Jones could plow over tacklers or out-sprint corners. Cascades' collection of receivers gave Prince the option to throw to any of them (us). Stew Shavers anchored aggressors who usually controlled the line of scrimmage.

And then there was me. What did the opposing coaches and players say about me? *He's goofy-looking . . . He runs patterns he rarely repeats . . . He lines up all over the formation . . . He can cut out, in and out again till he makes you dizzy . . . He has delicate hands that caress the ball into them . . . and when he turns on the jets you surely will suck his exhaust.*

I'm certain I was a puzzle to them. Strange name, strange gait, strange deployment in all facets of the Cascades' attack?

Our coaches weren't sure how New Cambria was preparing for us. Were their veteran coaches going to turn Cosmo "The Rifle" Clinksdale loose on our mostly untested secondary? Did they think they could control the clock with a ball-control running attack? Was their stalwart defense going to blitz us into oblivion?

Demon Dan told me I might have to play both ways, offense and defense.

"They've seen the havoc you can wreak," he said. "We might have to disguise when we'll use you. Might even sneak you in on a punt or kickoff return."

I confided to Ladarius, "Playoffs ratchet up the intensity, don't they?"

"You know it," he answered. "Even the bands sound better, cheerleaders jump higher, the stands rock louder. This is when high school football lives."

"Do you think we're ready, all of us who've never been here before . . ."

"Hey, this is what we were born to do. You think I sit in class all day and dream of solving quadratic equations?"

"I know what you mean. I really love Mr. Fasciola's American history. Yet there's nothing like the pandemonium that engulfs us when we run on the field at the beginning of a game."

"That's called buzz, man," said Ladarius. "I go to sleep most nights dreaming about that buzz. You probably hear pandemonium; I hear buzz."

"I like the anticipation, too. My nerves start to tingle as games get closer."

"Yeah, I wondered about you," said Ladarius. "You seem pretty cool when you unleash your speed. I couldn't tell if something inside you kicks in or what."

I hesitated. I wasn't sure if I should confess too much. "At the beginning, I didn't have the nervous tingle—what you call buzz. But now it comes, as the games get bigger. It is a great feeling, isn't it?"

"Well, some guys fold under the pressure."

I swelled my chest. "I won't. You know that, Lad, don't you? You know what you call buzz is slowly changing me. Do you think it'll make me better?"

"I sure hope so, man. You hold the key to unlock our destiny."

* * *

Callister Cascades vs. New Cambria was played on a bitterly cold night in early December. A snow squall had covered the field with a wet white coating. Coach didn't use me to return the opening kickoff. I had to admit I was disappointed. The buzz hummed in my head and joints. It had to stay pent-up till my chance came.

The stadium where we met was neutral, so neither of us had an advantage. Its turf was synthetic, which made it somewhat slippery with the moisture. Both teams tried to establish a running game at the beginning. Neither worked particularly well, with fumbled turnovers stopping drives on both sides.

Then the Rifle started firing bullets to all parts of the field—screens and dump-offs, down-and-outs, curls over the middle and posts that tested us deep.

Demon Dan sought me out early in the second quarter. "We're going to install you in a zone over the middle. Their big-time quarterback's getting full of himself. He's gonna go for the whole schmear down the field, and when he does, you be back there and break it up. Better yet, pick him off."

I had been playing long enough now that I could tell when the New Cambria ace was setting up a long "go" route. He threw a couple of passes underneath to his tight end, Knight, New Cambria's best receiver. Then he broke off his short route and blasted by me for a corner of the endzone.

"Bye-bye, Bubba," Knight goaded as he flew past.

I turned with him and ran step for step. The Rifle fired. The long arc was about to settle into Knight's sure hands when I reached in and took the ball away from him. I heard him grunt in surprise.

I returned the interception to the New Cambria twenty-five. Prince and Junius Jones did the rest. It was knotted 14-14 at halftime. Cambria seemed baffled. We were nine-point underdogs, and suddenly we were giving them all they could handle.

Coach Sawyer was buoyant in the locker room. "Boys, we're busting their bubble. The Rifle's firing a few blanks. We're gonna make some history."

Mr. Fasciola would have been proud. Three different mind pictures scrambled into a coaching omelet, topped by a reference to history no matter how weak.

When we came back onto the stadium apron at the start of the second half, the Callister Cascades band was still marching. Ladarius leaned into me. "Hear that beat—doesn't it stir your blood?"

Assistant Coach Sampson put a hand on my shoulder. His breath hovered above his short-sleeve T-shirt in the twenty-degree weather. "Sublimious, we're borrowing you on offense. When we get our shot, we're gonna use you to break this game open."

That stoked my buzz. I walked the sidelines, a heavy cloth cape draped over my shoulders. The third quarter came and went. Both teams scored a touchdown. I got in for a few plays, but my number wasn't called.

The game was tied 28-28 with the fourth quarter ticking down.

Okay, Mr. Sampson, I'm ready. I'm more than ready. I paced and paced. *What the hell are you waiting for?* I never cursed. Under my frozen breath, I apologized to my Emissary. He had counseled that anger was not part of the makeup of an explorer.

New Cambria punted to us. We started on our twenty-two with two and a half minutes left. I was inserted into the game with Ladarius and Styles at wide receiver. The first play was a sideline pass to Ladarius. The next was a short slant across the middle to Styles. Then a screen to tight end Heath. I was nothing but a decoy.

Finally, Prince looked me in the eye in the huddle and said, "Take off, Sub. Don't look back. The ball'll be there over your left shoulder at the goal line."

I was in the slot to the left, not even flanked wide like Ladarius and Styles. I sensed that the Cambria secondary paid me very little attention. Our coaches with their play selection had lulled them to sleep.

I hesitated one step off the line, then summoned Coach's jet-assisted rockets. I covered half the field in a golden blur. I looked up and, true to his word, Prince floated a cottony pass over my left shoulder. I had to reach for it, but my fingers felt every last pimple on that beautiful, hard leather surface.

When I looked back, there wasn't a New Cambria defender within fifteen yards of me. The crowd's roar totally engulfed me. I couldn't help myself. I tossed the ball to the ref, ran to the goalpost crossbar, leaped, and grabbed hold. I swung my whole self around the bar once. Then twice. Then a third time. I released and dismounted with a full double-tuck front flip.

MY GAWD, WHAT HAD I DONE! THE BUZZ HAD SEIZED ME AND TAKEN OVER! Ladarius stood beside me, shaking his head.

* * *

I had scored the winning touchdown. As the game-ending whistle sounded, I was swarmed, pounded, and declared a *hero*, an appellation I did not like or trust. Coach Sawyer embraced me and shouted in my ear, "That's what we were looking for, Zoo-flint-ius—scalding their fancy asses with one big cannon blast from those magic rockets!" His bizarre word paintings were beginning to grow on me.

One of my fellow receivers, Kadeem, yelled in my helmet's earhole, "Hey, man, you swingin' on the crossbar like an Olympic gymnastico! You teach me that?"

Others with wild grins called my impulsive whirligig original and death-defying. "Get us another win—you can jungle-swing all night."

I was being carried off the field in a flowing river of bodies. When I reached the entrance to the locker room, Ladarius blocked my path. "What were you doing out there? You make a big catch and pile it on with that goalpost gymnastics shit. Rules of the road, man. You can't do that crap and still be one of us."

People were pressing in so tight, I could barely breathe.

"Lad, honest, I forgot. The buzz you were talking about . . . the buzz got hold of me."

"You must remember, no preening like a peacock. No showboating. It'll separate you from the rest of us, and that'll be no good for the team."

I gripped Ladarius's arm. "You're right. I'll remember. I've got to remember."

* * *

The parking lot had emptied after Ladarius and I finished dressing. Mr. Drakos picked us up like usual. To my surprise, Samantha was in the back seat. I guess she was growing on Lad's dad—on all of us.

"I can't believe they let you do that, or that you did it. That monkey yo-yo."

Sam was laughing and bobbing her blonde bowl of a head.

"Refs called a penalty—you know that, don't you?" said Big Nico.

"No, I got lost in the moment," I replied. "My mind actually went blank."

"Sub's not going to do it again," Ladarius said sternly.

"Ah, why not?" Sam cackled. "It shows he's got some goans."

"'Cause it mocks the other team. Another thing, what if there's three minutes left and it gets us a fifteen-yard penalty? Then the other team starts on the forty."

Big Nico slapped the steering wheel. "I liked the hell out of it. Matter of fact, I think I'll put a wager down that he does it again next game."

He knew that was annoying to his son. He and Ladarius had strong ties, but I could detect chinks where they incited one another.

My phone in Sam's hands had been lighting up since we had left the parking lot. "Geez, you ought'a see all the posts you're getting from your closest thousand friends," she said.

"Should I answer them?" I replied. "That's the polite thing to do, isn't it?"

Sam punched me in the arm. "Man, you're such a dweeb. We could put a big emoji on your replies to everybody, and then they'll think you're just a sweet, dumb guy who friends even golden retrievers."

I leaned back in the dark insides of the car. This was complicated, more complicated than I wanted. I had done something that was instantly acclaimed in football—and I didn't quite know how to handle the after-effects of a foolish act that followed. I brooded, which I shouldn't have. But it was probably natural to someone so new to the game.

Mr. Drakos drove forty-five minutes to get from the game site to his restaurant in downtown Callister Cascades. He could barely find a parking spot when we arrived. "Whew, you guys are helping my bottom line on the nights you play. You're not expecting a cut of the action, are you?"

When we went inside, people started patting us on the shoulders and telling us what a great game we had played. "We ain't seen nothing like that in Cascades since I can remember," said one old man with an unkempt beard.

Customers were walking around with gyros in their hands, not even sitting in booths, but wanting to instead demonstrate their enthusiasm in some physical form. They offered to buy Ladarius and me any Greek specialties we wanted, as well as beer or wine. Mr. Drakos had to remind them he couldn't serve us alcohol.

"I have some weed in my handbag," said Sam. I knew she didn't because the last thing you'd find her with would be a handbag.

Girls from school and older women asked if Ladarius and I would take selfies with them. "You guys are really studly," a few said. "You sorta look worn out, though. Guess you won't be up to going home with us tonight."

Lad might have been studly, whatever that meant. I knew I wasn't. I looked in the mirror occasionally, and I'd see an ungainly, knock-kneed, gold-hued giraffe. I was sure my appearance worked in my favor on the football field. A defender would size me up and say to himself, *He can't be that fast, that elusive, that coordinated.* And then I'd throw a move on him, whirl by him, and snatch a pass from his hands, and he'd say, *Maybe I'd better watch him—looks can be deceiving.*

Sam and I sat in a back booth as she exclusively operated my cellphone. "We'll send everybody who has contacted you tonight a giddy, happy-face text thanking them for their felicitations."

"Yes, *felicitations.* I like that word. Send it with an emoji."

"I'll tell them when you see them in the hall on Monday, they can expect a high-five. Just be prepared to whack hands."

"But how can I possibly know all these people when I see them?"

"You know, Sub," Sam sighed, "you really are in your own world. It's why you hang with me. You don't know any better."

"That's what Lad tells me. However, I do know better. I simply like you. You are an off-the-wall accessory."

"Yeah, you mean a trophy bitch."

12

Then Monday at practice, Coach Sawyer pulled me aside and told me that he was going to install an offense in which I was the catalyst. "We've only used you in boom times. Now we want you to play more snaps. Teams in the playoffs from here on out are kick-ass. We need your speed to give us an edge."

He turned me over to Demon Dan. He was the one who'd worked with me on covering Burner Bormelo in the Thanksgiving game. He was relentless. Dan was going to teach me everything in the Callister Cascades receiving kitbag: slants, comebacks, curls, digs and drags, fades, corners, posts. I had to learn all the different wideout positions—flanker, slot, aligned in the backfield next to Prince, and motion behind the line of scrimmage.

"Before you were just running 'gos' and posts, simply using your speed to burst past defenders and get separation," Dan said. "Now you gotta know where all our other receivers are to find your open spaces. You must be there and ready because Prince will have the ball out before you even turn around."

He made me stay after practice. Made me watch film. Made me memorize alignments so I knew everybody's assignment. Filled me to absolute overflow.

"I can't remember all this," I protested. "Why don't you put me in one spot?"

"'Cause by using you all over, they won't know where to look for you."

"Yeah, but I just want to deploy my speed. That's what I came here to do."

Demon Dan stopped in his tracks. "What do you mean, 'Came here to do'?"

"Ah, you know, why I tried out for the team the first day I arrived."

Sometimes I stepped in it. I had brought my lightning from another place, and that was my secret to immediate success. I didn't mean for my gift to shine so brightly. It might give away too much.

"Look, you got to learn all this stuff, all these routes and responsibilities, so you'll be more valuable to the team. That's the only way we'll beat these very good teams coming up. Each player contributes to the max."

"Yes, yes, you're right. Teach me everything. I will implant it in my brain so my physical self can carry it out."

Demon Dan would stare at me for half a minute after I'd make such a statement. I could see his own very supple brain whirling.

"You're not like the rest of our receivers," he said. "Or any other player I've ever been around. You're weirdly cerebral and can't help showing it."

"I don't mean to be. I want to fit in and help us win."

So, I went out and stood at all these positions, ran the same patterns until I carved a groove in the turf. "You can't wear me out," I'd josh with Dan.

I'd stay until the lights came on in the stadium, until dinnertime came and went. Dan would take me to eat afterward. To Burger King, the pancake house, the Sonic drive-in. He said Coach Sawyer gave him the money out of a small-change kitty in the school athletics fund.

Even as we ate, he'd go over plays with me. He'd draw them on a paper napkin. Then afterward, he'd ask if he could drop me off at my house.

"No, just at the 7-Eleven out on the pike," I'd tell him.

Dan Kerkegaard was a great teacher because he believed in the team and the player and how they fit together.

Yet there was another part to my receiver education that Dan couldn't teach me—and Ladarius could. That's because Lad saw the need when nobody else did. He knew that the more the coaches were going to use me, the less time it meant for some of our other receivers: Aurelius, Styles, Kadeem, Heath, Bottoms, Murphy, and Ladarius himself.

"Somebody else's time is going to be stolen. A few guys are going to yap. Maybe even I'm not going to play as much," Lad said. "It could drive a wedge between us. So far, we've divvied up time and gotten our share of targets. But if some of us play less, it could hurt our solidarity."

Lad talked to me at lunch, in his dad's restaurant. He said he was trying to be a diplomat, someone who kept peace among guys who thought very highly of their skills and abilities to change a game.

"They all think they can influence an outcome," he said. "You, you're the only one who really can."

Ladarius was the unofficial captain of the receivers. They came to him with problems, complaints, slights by the coaches, and jealousies that festered. He was the "fixer," the "go-between."

"I am willing to share more playing time," I told him.

"You don't understand. You're not the guy doling out the minutes."

"I've been watching pro football on TV," I said. "You know what a pass receiver does after he scores a touchdown? He brings all the other receivers together, even his offensive linemen, and they celebrate like they all scored."

"Yeah, now you're thinking." Lad gave me a thumbs up. Then he added, "Another thing. In practice, ask the other receivers questions. You're new; they've all been around. Ask how they run a down-and-out or a slant. What's their secret? Then they think they're the expert and you're just copying them. When you come back to the huddle, you ask, 'How'd I do?'"

"I can puff out my chest and say, 'Now I run it like you, like the best.'"

"Okay, but try to be subtle. Sometimes you're too eager."

Ladarius had been playing football since he was five, in what was called the Pee Wee League. He was seventeen, a senior now. He said he was always learning: How to push off and get away with it. How to drag a foot after catching a pass before going out of bounds. How to rub a linebacker off to get another guy open.

The other Ram receivers had been playing a long time, too. I hadn't. I had to show deference to them and then—*maybe only then*—they'd accept me being awarded more playing time.

It was tricky, I knew. This game I'd chosen—that was actually chosen for me—was not easy. In addition to brawn and blow-by, you had to have brains. It was coming slowly, but sometimes I had to learn fast. I didn't have the benefit of twelve years like Ladarius did. I needed him, Demon Dan, and all my fellow receivers to let me know how to become a trusted teammate.

* * *

In the second playoff game against Shawnee Rock, I played every down in the first half. It was a tight defensive battle. I ran short and medium routes. I went in motion and caught screen passes. I was a decoy and blocker on sweeps by Junius Jones. On one play, Ladarius caught a pass in the flat and lateraled the ball to me as I got up a head of steam. A defensive lineman hit me so hard I almost fumbled.

At the end of the half, we trailed 7-6. We'd generated only two field goals.

Coach Sawyer confided softly in a corner of the locker room, "You're doing fine, Boo-lim-ious. The Rock's covering you tight as tits in a steel bra. We're going to cut you free when the time's right."

Ladarius and I leaned into each other and spoke quietly. "You see what the game plan is," he said. "You're running short, basic stuff. Rock may not even know you have speed 'cause it's being kept under wraps."

"How 'bout our guys? Any feedback about me playing so much?"

"Not that I sense. Game's too tense and everyone's locked in."

Midway through the second half, I ran a down-out-and-up to test the corner covering me. He bit on my first move and I broke clear on the second, but Prince didn't see that I was open and threw to another receiver.

When I came back to the huddle, I nodded to Prince: *I can beat him.*

Our quarterback stored that nod away.

On our next set of downs, he called the play on which I had come free. I ran it with precision and broke loose. Prince lofted a thirty-yard bomb down the right sideline, and just as I reeled it in, the Shawnee safety came out of nowhere and rattled me so hard I dropped the ball.

He stood over me and said, "Saw you run that before—better not run it again."

I stumbled to my feet, stars danced in my head.

On the sidelines, Demon Dan blustered, "Shit, we didn't account for him."

"Well, you better," I mumbled.

I sat out one sequence, waiting for the stars to stop circling the planets.

Ladarius sidled up next to me. "You okay? You probably got your bell rung. Hang in there—we're headed to the finish line."

Next time we had the ball, Coach Dan signaled me back onto the field. He grabbed me by the elbow and hollered, "That big safety is laying for you. This time drive ten yards, stutter-stop, and then take off and leave him to count his hangnails."

Yeah, Dan, if my legs stop shaking!

Prince called the play and whispered to me as we broke the huddle. "I'm going to pump once to suck that big galoot in, then you throw it in gear."

I remembered enough from Dan's repeat drills during the week. Head might not have been totally clear, but the repetitions had made their impression: Go hard straight at him, turn to freeze him, and then jam it into overdrive.

The safety bit for a split-second at my hesitation-stop. Then he tried to grab me and ended up with a handful of tear-away jersey. I was by him and gone. Prince laid the pass in my hands with a sharp sizzle that matched my flyaway gait. I glided across the goal line, but I hardly knew where I was.

It was rote. Muscle memory. Hands held a football high above the head, but it was all on automation. I had sprinted seventy yards downfield, so it took a few seconds for my teammates to catch up.

Ladarius gathered us. All the receivers. Beneath the goalposts. Arms around each other, we rolled the dice, signifying our big score. I'd done it, but *we'd* done it together. That was how Lad wanted it to appear, for the unity of our brotherhood.

I hardly remembered the score or celebration when I felt Demon Dan squeeze me in his arms as I was transported to the sidelines by my teammates.

Little time remained in the game. I did remember looking up at the scoreboard. I thought it was blinking. "Tell me, Lad, tell me, is that us with the 20, them with the 14?" I asked as we floated off the field in a sea of Callister Cascades jerseys. It seemed my feet never touched the ground.

"Yeah, we did it. But you're going to need some help. Stick with me."

I did. I had to. He had an arm wrapped tight around my shoulders as he lugged me to the locker room.

* * *

"Man, you broke it. You left that big axe-man safety sucking wind," yelled Kadeem. "What we needed, you delivered."

Prince whacked me on the shoulders. "He went for the pump fake, didn't he?"

Teammate after teammate came up, shook or slapped hands, shoved me in the chest, yelled something loud and crazy into the ceiling tiles.

I caught some, but not much. The room seemed bright and swirling. Ladarius gently lifted me off a bench and guided me into an office where he said the team doctor wanted to see me.

"Great game, Mr. Clancy," said Doc Sears. "Do you remember the last few plays?"

My mouth was so dry I could hardly speak. "Scoreboard was winking. We had the bigger number, at least that's what Lad told me."

"Well, that's a start."

He then asked a series of questions, a few of which I could answer. He conducted an eye exam and then checked my strength, balance, coordination, and reflexes. Most of the testing, though, seemed like it was on someone standing outside of me. I was merely an observer.

"How is he, Doc?" I heard Ladarius ask.

"He's had a concussion, a traumatic brain injury. It's an unfortunate risk factor in this game, we can't eliminate. I'm surprised there aren't more."

"What's it mean?" asked Ladarius. He was acting as my translator.

"The brain is suspended in fluid inside the skull. When a sudden blunt force causes the soft brain tissue to crash into the hard skull, it leads to inflammation or bruising of the brain, and the nerve tissues stretch. Hard to say how serious it is, but we must treat it as serious because the brain controls everything important in us."

"So, what does Sublimious do? How's he get better?"

"He must stay quiet, removed from most stimulus for at least twenty-four hours, hydrate with plenty of water, rest and sleep. No football or practice until I see him again. Pretty much stay out of the regular flow of school and contact for a few days. I realize that may be difficult after his heroics today, but it's the only way he'll recover in a reasonable amount of time."

I heard them talking, but for some reason, I thought they were talking about someone else. Ladarius helped me back into the locker room, where I slowly dressed. All the players had boarded the bus for the trip back to school.

Coach Sawyer was waiting for us. Ladarius explained Doc Sears's diagnosis. "Well, that sounds like a bummer," Coach blustered. "We got a championship in two weeks. You think Blu-blim-ious will have his head cleared out and ready to play?"

"It depends on whether Sub can rest and heal and whether Doc pronounces him fit to go," said Ladarius. I stood next to him like a cardboard cutout. *Sure,*

sure, you can count on me, I wanted to say. But I could barely think of the words, any words, that might reassure Coach.

Ladarius's dad had permission from the staff to drive me home.

"To your place, to Drakos," I mumbled. I had to go to their restaurant, I knew. I couldn't return to a small rented house where I was presumed to live with my grandfather. I sensed I'd be virtually helpless. I hoped Lad and his dad could find someplace quiet for me. I was totally dependent on them getting me where I had to be.

* * *

At the Drakos restaurant, Ladarius and his dad led me into a storage room below the main dining area. It had shelves piled high with cans, jars, plastic bins, and three huge freezers. They said they'd find a cot, plenty of blankets, and pillows for an overnight stay or longer. I could hear the faint rumble of voices and footsteps in the restaurant above.

"There will be plenty of drinking and carrying on upstairs," said Big Nico. "But you won't hear much of it. There's good insulation in the floor."

I lay stretched out and stared at the ceiling. I had never felt so different or detached. The Keyslan powers-to-be spoke of possible injury. I was to play a violent sport. But they spoke of broken bones or Achilles tendon tears, not invisible injuries that robbed functioning thought.

"I can't play for a while?" I inquired of Lad.

"Not until Doc clears you."

"That can't be. We've got a big game, right?"

"State championship. The biggest."

"So I've got to be able to play. This is why I am here."

"What do you mean, 'why you're here'? It's why all of us are here. Callister Cascades never expected it in a million years. Now we're only one win away."

I lay back. With my brain enmeshed in fog, I sensed danger. I was in a new region that I hadn't prepared for. I was being told I had to turn everything off. Shut down until my brain could be in command again.

"Lad, can I stay? Can I curl up and stay until you tell me it's safe?"

"Sure, you don't have to go anywhere. You can rest and sleep. We'll bring you food. You eat as much or as little as you like. If you sleep right through the night, you may feel a lot better in the morning."

That was when I heard another voice. Samantha Schneider had found us. She came bulling into the storage room, took one look at me, and backed off.

"Geez, for a guy who saved the day, you look like a wreck," she announced.

"The school taking the win okay?" I tried to joke.

"You shittin' me? Upstairs there's wall-to-wall people marinating in beer and souvlaki. I'll bet the rest of the town's ready to blow. They'd erupt if you ever showed your face, but you ain't about to do that, are you?"

Sam sat down on the old couch where I lay. "The question is, what do I tell your million friends trying to get through to you on their devices?"

She crowded in on me in her fur coat and jeans. Her gloved hands rested on my blanketed chest. "Maybe I should tell 'em you've gone to the other side and will be back in a week."

Sam looked fresh, scrubbed. I smiled and asked if she'd be my nurse.

"Please, you don't want that. I've got no bedside manner."

"Should we tell all the Ram fans that Sublim's been hurt?" she asked Lad. "They'd expect to see him after he turned the game around like he did."

"I'd put it out there he's unavailable," he said. "But don't say anything about a concussion. Just say it's an injury that requires rest."

"That okay with you?" Sam asked me. "You're hurt. You're going to rest all weekend. Tell them to celebrate and knock themselves out. Maybe they'll figure that's what you did to yourself."

"Yeah . . . I guess. You guys know best."

I kept drifting and drifting. Lad and his dad brought in a cot, blew up an air mattress, got me into some borrowed sweat clothes, threw at least three blankets over me, and turned out the lights. I heard nothing.

I heard and did nothing most of Saturday. Ate a meal of eggs, toast and hot tea. Then I slept some more. Woke up on Sunday with the fog mostly gone. My head still hurt, but I felt I was slipping back into the real world again. I wanted to go upstairs to the restaurant and have a gyro.

To Ladarius and his dad, that was a good sign. I actually ate two gyros with a lemonade. Sam came, and we sent out a catch-all post: "I'm feeling much better. Thanks for the concern and well wishes from all Callister Cascades' friends and believers. Our team is headed for greatness."

I listened to music on Pandora for the rest of Sunday.

13

By Sunday evening, I felt close to normal again. I ate a real meal. I played *Call of Duty* with Ladarius. I stayed out of the way, hidden, even though Sam said I had a thousand phone messages. Coach Sawyer didn't know where I was. I had Sam send him a brief text saying I'd be at practice on Monday.

Ladarius asked if I wanted to go home to my grandfather's, so I could see my parents on weekends. I lied to him that they were traveling on an assignment. He never probed any further. He and his dad told me I could stay in my Drakos hideaway for as long as I liked.

I knew I couldn't face school on Monday. There would be too many questions about what had happened, if it was serious, and if I would be able to play in the championship.

Sam said she could send out a photo. "I could make you look like a complete goober, holding up a V for victory with two fingers."

"Whoa, I'm afraid of how I look normally."

"Hey, all they know is they didn't see Sublimious Clancy for a brief while. They want to know if you'll be back for this most gigantist game of all our lives."

On Monday afternoon, I asked Mr. Drakos to drop me off near the practice field. I wanted to meet the coaches and team without having to walk through school. My brother receivers were happy to see me. So was Prince: "You gonna be ready? You'll be able to run a couple more blue streaks, right?"

Coach Sawyer greeted me with a back slap. "You look put back together.

Hope Doc Sears gives you a clean bill of health." He then assembled the whole squad in the gym.

"Boys, I'm so proud of what you did Friday night that I'm bursting my inseams. We got one more game—a big game, a huge game—a humongous shootout at O.K. Corral. That's what my scouts and film crew tell me. The Allendale High Avalanche won their Western semifinal 49-41. Man, sounds like we got a track meet on our hands."

Coach was pacing. For some reason, he was wearing cleats on a wood floor.

"They spread the ball around like it's hot jam on toast. Got two six-foot-five receivers, the brothers Grimm, who'll either smash you in the mouth or outsprint you. Their quarterback slings the ball to all parts of the yard, and he puts it through tiny windows. He'll have us scrambling, but we'll find a way to plug up those windows."

He was pacing and clicking. "Defense, they don't play much. It's bend-but-don't-break. If we break it more than they bend, we'll beat 'em. We'll be proud forever. You know, you'll be able to walk around Cascades downtown and people will buy you burgers and Dr Peppers for a year. Maybe a lifetime."

Coach held up a book. Nobody could read the title. "Boys, I never dreamed at the beginning of this year that we had a chance to be in the history books. Tarnation, we got a real shot. Your names will be writ down in these pages in bold color. Forty years from now, you can come walking in here on canes and you'll be able to look it up. STATE CHAMPIONS! You can show your kids and grandkids, and they'll ask what it was like to win it all."

"Geez," Ladarius whispered to me. "Coach already has us old men."

When the team left for the practice field, Coach called me over. "Bi-lim-ious, you gotta go see Doc Sears. Tell him your head's emptied out of all the bad voodoo. You're ready to strap it on and enter the history books."

Doc was glad to see me upright, eyes clear, voice even. He asked more questions, did a few tests. "No signs of any after-effects," he assessed. "You got pretty well dinged Friday night. I want you to ease back in."

"My teammates are out practicing. I've got to be with them."

"You can be with them. I just don't want any contact, serious physical exertion, or even goofing around with them for at least a week. You can do light calisthenics, ride an exercise bike, and participate in walk-throughs. But nothing else till I say so."

"My head's clear, sir. I don't want any special treatment," I said.

"Mr. Clancy, your brain takes a good one to three weeks to heal after an observable concussion. I'll check with you again at the end of the week. Then I'll decide whether you can play or not."

"But I've got to play. It's why I'm here. That's why I started playing at this high school at the beginning of this football year."

"Well, I've never heard it put quite that way. You make it sound like life or death."

"It's just the way it is... in my mind, at least."

"In my mind, however, I'm paid to protect players. And that's what I'm going to do, even though I know how important you've been to this team's success."

*   *   *

Word somehow got out that my chances of playing in the championship were only fifty-fifty. I was pretty sure Doc Sears didn't release any statement. Maybe it was hearsay from some of the players who saw me doing only light workouts. But now virtually everybody in the school and the town knew I'd had a concussion.

"You don't push it when your brain's involved," advised Burke Pennypack, leader of the school's e-sports league. "I might have to take you out of my game-day lineup. I can't afford to risk further serious injury."

"Burke," I protested, "you're only playing electronic games."

"But you go down early, I'm stuck with an untested receiver I can't trust."

Burke's dilemma mirrored how the rest of the school and town felt. Students stopped me in the hall to tell me I had to play. This was the biggest game of the year, of all their school-age years—even the biggest of the century, for goodness' sake.

Every store in town had large signs in their windows: RAMS BRING DOWN THE AVALANCHE . . . WIN ONE MORE, WALK TOGETHER FOREVER . . . CALLISTER CASCADES, HOME OF CHAMPIONS.

The sporting goods store even had a picture of Prince at one end of a large bay window and me, Sooblimious Clancy (they spelled it wrong), at the other end with a football rigged on an electric pulley to soar between us. Sam said she was going to sneak in and draw a mustache and a tattoo on my image to make me look more hunky.

"You know it's like this little poof-burg of a town is about to do something the rest of America is going to stand up and pay attention to," mocked Sam. "The president's gonna come and toss the coin at midfield and present the championship trophy to the winner. I wonder if the local airport can handle Air Force One."

Each day, I'd go to team practices, but I wasn't allowed to run or flag passes or go through blocking drills. Demon Dan was given the assignment to work with the quarterbacks and receivers. I could monitor the pass routes and alignments the coaches were putting in for the game. However, I couldn't run or even jog.

"Hey, we don't want you tripping over one of the stripes on the field," joked Kadeem. "We gonna have to make do without you. Don't know if we can do it."

I knew my brothers were teasing. Yet I couldn't help but feel there was an ounce of harsh judgment behind their ribbing. They were the old hands, guys who had been there shagging Prince's passes for years. I had come out of nowhere, stealing their thunder. Now I was wrapped in cotton, and they didn't have much sympathy.

Every student, townie and coach was worried about *me*—not *them*. They were going to play, but the sole question anybody asked: Was Sublimious in for the count?

In the midst of all this doubt, Mr. Fasciola suggested we have lunch again. He brought the sandwiches this time: cheese steaks with onions and peppers.

He smiled as he unwrapped the foil. "I'll probably fall asleep halfway through my one o'clock class after eating one of these monsters."

"Don't worry, nobody'll notice," I joked.

"Last time we convened for lunch, I did my history spiel about the evolution of football, didn't I?" began Mr. Fasciola.

"That seems to be what I remember."

"All my so-called insights into the meritocracy of who gets to play and how the all-American buck influences the game. I probably sounded like your typical pompous history teacher."

"No, no, I love to hear your perspective. I need to learn as much about this game from someone who knows the lore."

Mr. Fasciola took a large bite of his steak, juice sluicing down his chin. "Sometimes I think all you're doing is buttering me up," he chuckled.

"Oh, why would I do that? I'd put the butter on something edible."

My teacher shook his head. "I know you're not as naive as you imply."

He took a drink of soda. "You see how this town and this school relate to this upcoming football game," he said. "It's as if there is nothing more important to our entire existence. That's not reality, is it? It gives people something they can wrap their heads and hands around. Something tangible, graspable, I guess."

"Yes, I've begun to see such total immersion."

"So you've been injured. I don't know exactly the kind of injury, but I suspect it might involve the head. That's nothing to take lightly. And now you have all this pressure to play. You're vital to the team and this game—and you are, there's no denying that. But make sure you do what's best for you. You can listen to all the hopes and dreams of others. It's really between you and the team doctor to decide your playing condition and nobody else."

"I'm aware of that, sir. You don't know how much I appreciate hearing from someone impartial... or outside the loop, as they say."

Mr. Fasciola looked me in the eyes. His eyes were very dark and penetrating. I couldn't avoid them, nor the message behind them.

"The football culture puts a lot of stress on any player, especially one coming back from injury. People are clamoring for you to get back out on the field. If you do, you're celebrated for your toughness. Even the team doctor is under pressure to get someone like you cleared and ready. Especially in a game of this magnitude for our school and all of Callister Cascades."

I assured him, "Doc Sears will decide by the end of this week, so I've heard."

"He'll be fair, I'm sure. I can imagine all the advice he's fielding... 'Sublimious has to play; he spells the difference.' That's what everyone is telling him. Whew, I'm glad I don't have to make the choice."

I finished my steak sandwich. "I'm starting to understand how so many people feel. In all honesty, sir, I can't be that important, really. But I know what this game means to so many, and I guess my recovery is at the heart of it."

"And, hey, win or lose, you can always doze off in my American history class when the season ends."

"It is a very enticing invitation... after accomplishing what I have to do."

* * *

The Emissary asked to see me. I had gotten word that Doc Sears had approved me to practice at full strength during the week leading up to the championship game on Saturday.

"Zoo-blim-ious, now your head can fill with fly routes instead of the dance of gingerbread nutcrackers," said Coach Sawyer when he saw me.

I'd stayed in the storage room of the Drakos for more than a week. Even after

I was cleared to play, Big Nico and Ladarius told me I didn't have to leave. "I've gotta take care of my investment," Lad's father confessed when we were alone. "I put a nice tidy bet down on the Rams with a couple of money bags I know. We're the underdogs, so I'm getting points."

I wanted so badly to say, "You can't do that to Lad. He's told you how much he hates you gambling on him, *us*." But I held my tongue; they were my protectors.

At midweek, I went to the safe house out on the edge of the Gates of Wisdom Forest. The Emissary wanted an update. I could sense vibrations surrounding me in the small, bare room.

Sublimious... came the mellifluous voice after minutes. *I'm afraid we have put you in a delicate position, from what the Oracles tell me. You've suffered a head wound that leaves you in a questionable limbo as to whether you are allowed to participate in a contest critical to your team, school, and community. Do we have the facts of the matter correct?*

"Yes, sire. However, I've been permitted to play. I plan to join my teammates in a game of substantial significance to all of us."

I heard a stirring. It sounded like a creak in the ceiling, as if the beams were straining from a heavy weight set upon them.

The question we would ask: Is that wise in this new environment in which you've been placed? Are you being subjected to a potential conflict in your assignment that goes beyond what is ultimately beneficial to us Keysians?

I paused to think. I did not wish to give an unmeasured response.

"I have come this far in my exploration of football. It has far surpassed what I expected. I see how important it is in the school and community we have chosen... and I've become important in the success of our team. In this ultimate confrontation, I will see how these two matters come together," I replied.

So your worlds collide, so to speak.

"I trust I can avoid a collision like I had that momentarily incapacitated me. If I can, then I remain valuable to everyone around me. That is my goal: to contribute. And then when I get my opportunity, to unveil my special powers."

The Emissary's vent of steam turned to what sounded like a heavy sigh. *Oh, yes, special powers. We equipped you with the extraordinary talent of speed. We've always told you to be careful: deploy it at the right time, or you will become what the Americans term beyond the pale, a suspect in their eyes.*

"Yes, they have a term for it: A nail that sticks out too far needs to be pounded in. I do not wish to become that nail," I said.

I felt the vibrations around me become more pronounced.

If you can succeed, if you overcome this head wound, then all your American acquaintances will see the strength and value of Keysians, and we can fit more seamlessly if the tipping point ever materializes for when we must assimilate.

"My contribution will not be easy. This game is challenging; the participants are tough and unyielding. The people who follow us are extremely demanding. I must strive to reach a height where I satisfy all these expectations."

The last sound I think I heard was a faint hurrah, maybe even a hallelujah.

And Sublimlous, remember: Win one for the Emissary!

PART THREE

Choices

14

THE STATE CHAMPIONSHIP GAME WAS TO BE PLAYED ON A COLLEGE campus in a large stadium that held about forty times more fans than did our modest Callister Cascades football field. It was scheduled for the Saturday before the holiday known as Christmas. As I learned, that occasion heralded a miracle: A child of God born to poor parents in an animal stable that would over the millennia change human history.

I was aware the game fell about ten stratospheres below the significance of that sacred event. But to some in our school and community, it eclipsed ordinary life for at least that week leading up to it and that day on which it fell.

Sam told me that the nearest momentous event was an explosion at the largest plant in town, where a company made aviation fuel for airlines. It was horrific, she said, with six lives lost. It was years ago. This game was *now*. Lives would not be lost, but the fixation on our game would be just as intense.

"We've never been here before," said Sam with a derisive snarl. "Families put the gravity of the game somewhere between winning the zillion-dollar lottery and losing their house to the bank. You're not feeling it, though, are you, Sub-baby?"

"Oh, I've been cleared to play. I just need to strap on my jetpacks."

"That sounds like some malarky Coach Sawyer has fed you."

"Have you been spying on our locker room, Samantha?"

"No, I've seen too many sports movies where the coach looks his players in the eye and tells them they'll remember this game for the rest of their lives."

"My gosh, Sam, Coach Sawyer's done that too."

"I'm telling you," she laughed, "football is one big colossal cliché."

Talk of the game was on local TV, on all the social media platforms, and in all the shops and restaurants (especially Drakos) along Main Street. The schools, from high to elementary, were hung with the Cascades colors of gold and blue streamers, placards urging bold victory, even full-sized pencil sketches of team members drawn by an award-winning school artist. Townies, who largely ignored students the rest of the year, smiled, waved, and indicated *the game* mattered as much as newborn babies and family reunions.

One Callister Cascades graduate who had made it big with the Grand Ol' Opry in Nashville returned to give a free midweek concert. Other alumni who had gone on to bigger and better things came back and acknowledged their one-time connection to the school and the community. A special day was held mid-week when all municipal and business employees were given paid time off to attend a rally in the National Guard armory. Bands played, color guards marched, cheerleaders leaped, and the mayor read a proclamation that declared our team one of "ordinary athletes who did the extraordinary." Shop owners, supermarkets, fast-food chains, and restaurants agreed to give team members half-price discounts for a month.

The high school even held a special assembly the day before the game. Coaches and the team sat on an elevated stage and listened to the superintendent of schools tell us that we'd given a "heroic patina" to a hundred-year-old school that had been rejuvenated with a robust competitive vigor. Coach Sawyer admitted he'd never met the superintendent before and thought that patina meant "old cruddy flecked paint." Once the super sat down, others, such as a teacher, the head of student council, the yearbook editor, and even a favorite custodian, gave rousing speeches punctuated by fists in the air and cheers that nearly brought the house down.

"Gawd, the roof's going to blow off this place!" Ladarius shouted to me.

"You think we can live up to all this fire and fury?"

After the assembly let out and school was dismissed because everyone was too hyped up, we Rams had a walk-through on a cold outdoor field. Coaches told us we had to get used to the weather; tomorrow's forecast was twenty-five degrees with snow flurries. "When you get smacked the first time," Coach said, "we don't want you fragmenting like a busted icicle."

Demon Dan took the QBs, receivers and running backs onto a separate part of the field and told us we had to be at our absolute "pinnacle peak." He explained, "Allendale's offense is going to throw the kitchen sink, along with the living room and attic, at us. We've gotta match 'em down for down, score for score for four quarters and maybe even longer. They, my friends, are the real deal."

We all looked at one another with a steely resolve. "We can do it," Ladarius told all of us. "We've been doing it all year. Shocking the world. Why not one more time?"

We stacked hands around Dan's powerful arm, held like an umbrella pole in the center. "Tonight, dream victory," he chanted. "Tomorrow, bring it home!"

*　*　*

I slept one more night in the Drakos storage room, made ultra-comfy with a space heater. We rose at 5 a.m. and Big Nico fed us a solid all-American breakfast with hot coffee, which neither of us usually drank. He drove us to the team bus, which was a luxury coach that left at 6:30 and arrived at the neutral college stadium at 9:00.

We disembarked and then donned stripped-down uniforms for a light work-out on the most cushioned turf I'd ever been on. Then we adjourned to a high-tech locker room like none of us had ever seen. It had cool, mint-green lighting with huge leather chairs in front of each self-cleaning locker with cellphone chargers and hydration stations. We looked at each other and shook our heads.

"Hey, maybe we should hole down in here," said Aurelius, "and phone the game in."

Ladarius elbowed me. "Most of us can only dream of playing at a university like this. Maybe someday *you* can."

I didn't comprehend exactly what he was talking about. I was here for *this year*, probably no other. But the environment was seductive.

When we went out onto the field for pregame warm-ups, we noticed buses, minivans, and cars piling into the parking lot. Callister Cascades was arriving full-force: the band, cheerleaders, color guard, special card sections in the stands, parents and townies in school jackets, old returning graduates.

I spotted Sam the Slam at one corner of the fence surrounding the field. She introduced me to her mom in a knee-length leopard-print coat. She had never been to a football game in her life. "She has a flask of gin rickeys with her, in case she gets bored," said Sam. "She ain't going to get bored sitting next to me."

Burke Pennypack waved from the stands. He had a huge shoulder-mounted camera. He told me beforehand he'd be filming the game and converting it somehow to an electronic video game. He had humbly vowed to make me an e-sport "star."

Coach Demon Dan pulled me aside immediately before kickoff and said to be ready for anything. "We might need you here and there on defense to stop their jumbo ends. Might throw you in on a kickoff or punt return to keep them on their toes. Set up bubble screens or shovel passes to keep their linebackers honest. All sorts of routes from buttonhooks to bombs to start rocks falling on the Avalanche."

I stood next to Ladarius as both schools' bands played the American national anthem. My hands were over my heart, but I thought of the Emissary and all the Keysians whom I'd be representing. As the last words drifted into the air, "O'er the land of the free and the home of the brave," I whispered, "I can't let them down."

"Who?" Lad murmured back.

"Ah... everyone," I muttered.

"You won't."

My eyes roved around the large bowl of a stadium. It was nearly full. Allendale had packed its side. Its fans were as strident as ours. I was not on the field for the kickoff, but I heard the impact of bodies and winced. It instantly brought home the hit from the Shawnee Rock safety.

Once the game got rolling, I totally forgot about possible injury and became caught up in the action. Bodies flew and rammed into one another. Curses rose from piles of grunting humanity. Refs blew whistles and marched off penalties. I caught a pass over the middle and was flattened. I jumped up immediately to prove that even the most punishing hit couldn't hurt me.

I noted the game seemed to be going at another speed. I was fast, but so was everybody around me. The weight of the game had kicked in, and every player was digging deep for the breakthrough that might tilt the momentum.

Allendale had been in state championships before. We'd heard they were brash and tough because their brothers and cousins and maybe even fathers had played in games of this magnitude. Their quarterback, Jake Paretsky, was headed for a big-time SEC program and then the pros. He had twin-brother receivers, Hal and Hody Grimm, who caught passes and ran like road-graders. Their defense wasn't supposed to be any more than adequate, yet its hits were still thunderous.

We told ourselves we weren't going to be intimidated. "Come on!" roared Coach, "They pull their pants on one leg at a time. We ain't coming here to get bumified and bamboozled!"

We knew what to expect. But Junius Jones lost a fumble deep in our own territory. Prince threw a pick-six. My fellow receivers and I developed stone hands, and we couldn't sustain any drives. Right before halftime, the Allendale punt returner sprinted through our entire coverage team for a seventy-eight-yard touchdown run.

As we walked off the field and entered the tunnel for the locker room, our fans stared down at us from their seats, stunned. They wanted to know if we'd even shown up. "You guys are zombies!" one yelled. "We didn't come all this way to be embarrassed. Get your heads out of your asses and show 'em what Callister Cascades is made of!"

The locker room was silent. Steam poured off us, and we seemed to be shrinking. The coaches stood with their hands in their pockets and paced the plush, padded carpet. Finally, after many mute minutes, Ladarius walked to the center of all the slumping shoulders and said in a quiet, determined voice: "This is not how we want to be remembered. We came this far. We came from nothing. Our school, our town, loved us because we played with heart and commitment nobody'd ever seen before. We go out in this next half and play like it's our last hour of existence. If we do that, we can at least walk off that field like we shot our full wad and couldn't reach for one more ounce of sweat and spark and throat spittle."

None of us was willing to concede. We all picked our heads up, nodded to each other, and muttered, "Yeah, why not? If they kill us, we'll at least die bleeding blood and guts."

As we went back out through the tunnel and onto the field, we heard our stands erupt. The full-throat cheering washed over us and made our spines tingle. The Cascades fans hadn't given up on us, and now we couldn't either.

"You hear that, Rams?" bellowed Coach. "Our people know we have the cajones to come back."

But the scoreboard didn't lie: We were down 32-7.

* * *

The second half began auspiciously. Prince chucked a near interception that Styles wrestled away from one of the giant Grimms. He took it to the Allendale thirty-three, and we pounded it in on six plays. Stew Shavers and our defensive line stiffened and stopped the Avalanche on a three-and-out. Demon Dan huddled with Prince and the wide receivers. "Run screens and short turn-ins," he ordered. "Put them in a snooze, then burn them with Sublim down the right sideline."

I felt flames roar from my heels as I wheeled thirty-five yards without looking up. When my eyes lifted, the pass virtually rested on my left shoulder. My Allendale defender was five yards in my wake. Our sidelines awakened. We were high-fiving and pounding each other's shoulders. The Cascades' stands were rocking.

In the next series, we sacked their quarterback, Paretsky. Then he threw a short sideline pass to one of the Grimms. Our corner knocked him five yards into his own tumbling teammates. The big end threw a punch at one of our players. He'd been suckered into retaliation, and a ref tossed him from the game.

Allendale began to show a chipiness that told us doubts were creeping in.

Next time we had the ball, Coach called a slow-developing end-around. Just as it seemed Ladarius was about to be gang-tackled, he reared up and tossed a looping pass to me. It took an eternity to reach me, but when I latched on to it, I turned the jets on and scored. We'd cut the lead to 32-28, and the fourth quarter had barely started.

But the Avalanche was not about to fold. Paretsky and its high-powered offense gathered itself and scored. Suddenly, it was back to a 40-28 deficit. Maybe the mountain had been too high to climb. But Coach Sawyer and Demon Dan refused to let us quit. "You hear our people shoutin' themselves hoarse? You can't leave 'em to go home to gargle bourbon!" hollered Coach. His throat veins were bulging.

We started a drive with six minutes left. Prince was cool under fire. He hit all of us receivers on crossing patterns and in the open zone seams. Then he flicked a forward lateral to Junius Jones for a touchdown. We were now only down 40-35.

Our defense fought and clawed to force an Allendale punt with two minutes left. We had eighty yards to cover. The Avalanche dropped back into a full-scale prevent. Prince then chipped away with sideline down-and-outs to get us to the fifty.

At a timeout, Ladarius pulled me aside. He stared into my facemask and croaked, "You know all that stuff I said about rules of the road and respect for your teammates?"

I nodded.

"Well, forget it!" he hollered. "Do what comes into your ever-loving head that nobody's ever seen before. Forget what anybody thinks!"

"Yeah, you mean it?" I shouted back.

In the huddle, I told Prince to take a deep drop, count to five, and then throw the Wilson as far down the field as he could.

There were just nineteen seconds left on the clock.

I came off the line, did a full spin. Cut across the center, did another full spin the opposite way. Cut to the middle, cranked off a full-tuck cartwheel, landed, and threw it into high gear. I was practically dizzy from the spins and tumbles, but as I blew across the goal line, Prince had put a perfect arc on the ball. I reached up, snatched it clean, and blazed through the endzone.

Just six seconds remained.

We'd cut it as close as we possibly could.

Still, I could go and do three full-body loops around the goalpost crossbar.

No, no, no!

Ladarius didn't permit me to be a preening peacock. I strode quietly back toward our bench. On the scoreboard, we now had 41, Allendale 40.

Callister Cascades had shocked the world. Just as no one—and everyone who believed—had promised.

* * *

It felt like the whole massive university stadium had fallen in on top of us. Students and parents and townies and wide-grinning faces we'd never seen before swamped and swallowed us in a mass mob. I tried to hang on to Ladarius, but we got separated and carried to the far end of the field, where an elevated platform had been set up. I was deposited onto its steps and shoved upward into the arms of Coach Demon Dan.

"Hey, man, that final pass route, did we ever practice that before?"

Dan had wrapped me in his arms and was waltzing with me out onto the flat stage. Coach Sawyer shook my hand to the point I thought he was going to pry it off. Other people in suits were clapping me on the back and swearing they'd never seen a play like the last one. I learned they were members of the State Championship Coordinating Committee.

Then a woman stepped forward and presented a gleaming trophy in the shape of a football player. It looked more like Prince throwing a pass than me catching one. Coach accepted it, held it over his head, and shouted to the crowd below: "This belongs to you, Callister Cascades. When you brought us back onto the field in the second half with the roar of a thousand ram horns, we knew you hadn't quit on us. So we couldn't on you. And we didn't, did we?"

Coach Sawyer danced around the stage and almost dropped the football-player trophy. Aurelius lunged forward and caught it. "Thank God," yelped Coach, "that we got some sure-handed receivers."

Then a man in a long coat grabbed the microphone and said very coolly, "Folks, the Most Valuable Player Award has to go to the Callister Cascades wide receiver who made that last astounding play, but who also caught ten passes for 164 yards and three touchdowns... SUBLIMIOUS CLANCY!"

Someone pushed me forward. I practically collided with the man holding the award. He handed me a silver wreath with a sculpted football in the center. Like Coach, I practically dropped it. The man wanted to shake my hand. I fumbled and stuck my hand through the center of the prize. He said, smiling, "I can see you're more comfortable catching footballs on the field than trophies from an old man."

I hardly noticed, and neither did anyone else, but the snow flurries throughout the second half of the game now fell at a steadier rate. Everyone on the stage was covered in a white dusting.

Another guy, in an orange jacket and a brown walrus mustache, wrapped a big arm around me. He shoved a microphone shaped like a club in front of my face. "Sublimious . . ." he boomed. "Where'd you ever come by a name like that?"

I supposed he was somebody I needed to answer. "My parents must have thought I looked like a Sublimious," I replied.

"Well, what is a Sublimious, since you musta looked like one?"

"I think it means sublime or noble or something. You'd have to ask them."

"Are they here? Are they proud of their son being the MVP?"

"No, they're traveling." I was beginning to get nervous.

"Traveling? Maybe skiing somewhere?"

"They don't ski."

"I'm sure they'd be pleased as punch if they'd seen your outstanding game."

The orange-jacket man was waving the mic like a piece of fruit in front of me. "So I understand this is your first year of playing," he said, his mustache coated with snow. "How could you possibly get so good so fast?"

"By learning... and others teaching," I mumbled.

At this very moment, Ladarius saved me. He came forward arm-in-arm with Aurelius, Styles, Kadeem, Heath and Prince. "We all taught him," said Lad to the mustache man. They crowded together and embraced me. "Sublim came with the speed, and we pass-receiving compadres supplied the moves. He's a fast learner."

I retreated from the mustache man. I knew he had more to ask. Thankfully, my teammates weren't going to let him. I then threw the hood of my windbreaker cape over my head and slid down the steps of the platform. Samantha was waiting for me. I handed her my MVP trophy. "Will you keep this safe? I think it might be worth holding onto. I'll see you back at the Drakos."

Sam had her mother at her side. She looked very happy and impervious to the snow and cold. "Can Mom join us? She drank all her rickeys."

"Sure. She's a football fan now, right?"

"Oh, yeah. She thinks you're as big as Stone Cold Steve Austin."

*   *   *

We took the same bus that brought us home. All of us were wearing headphones and dancing to our own music. I listened to a prerecorded message from the Emissary. He had given me a sort of pep talk before the championship, urging me to play well and laying out a welcoming mat for the Keysians if ever came the need for migration. I had listened to it going to the game so that I understood the urgency of performing well. I'd achieved everything I set out to do.

Now I listened to the message again to judge whether I was done. Was I to be called home to report my most detailed findings? Or did I still have more to learn about American football and its impact on a town, an institution and a general population? Perhaps its impact even on myself?

I'd played for almost five months. I'd learned about being a teammate, taking orders, working as a unit, and fitting in. I had liked what I had seen and achieved. The friends I had made would be hard to leave. I'd been exposed to another culture, another way of thinking. It was leaving an imprint and changing me.

Could I tell the Powers that I wanted to stay, that I had more to learn? Might that just be an excuse? Callister Cascades was growing on me. Keysiana was my home, the only home I'd known. Now, however, I had become aware of other choices, new ideas and expanding possibilities. Was my Emissary the only source of wisdom? Could I think and decide for myself?

I leaned against the window of the luxury bus. Listened to the hum of the tires and the celebratory uproar around me. Closed my eyes and wondered.

15

THE BUS DROVE AROUND THE TOWN SQUARE AND DOWNTOWN AT LEAST a half dozen times. Callister Cascaders were out on the sidewalks and in front of the shops with their festive Christmas lights gleaming. It was twenty degrees with a light snow falling. No one cared about catching the flu or even freezing solid into an ice sculpture. People, kids, dogs were romping around, banging on the sides of the bus, throwing snowballs at its windows, honking their car horns.

"Never seen nothing like it," said Coach Sawyer. "People won't be this happy at my funeral."

The bus finally carried us back to our high school, where all the players' rides home were waiting. Big Nico picked up Ladarius and me and drove us to his restaurant. It was filled to overflowing. Nico had two cooks and a wait staff already at work. They were serving moussaka, souvlaki, beer, wine and liquor at a breakneck pace.

As soon as Lad and I walked in, people started cheering, clapping, chanting "MVP!" and asking for autographs on everything from placemats to their own clothing. They began blaring C-A-L-L-I-S-T-E-R C-A-S-C-A-D-E-S! For some, the name was too long or they began misspelling it. Many, most likely, had begun drinking in the stands from the start of the game.

Nico guided us to a booth in the rear, away from the milling throngs. Samantha Schneider was already seated there with her mother. They were eating from a smorgasbord of Greek dishes. Her mom had removed her leopard-print coat and was wearing a sleeveless sweatshirt with what appeared to be a multicolored archery target on the front. Her hair was chopped short, and I noticed earrings dangling with what seemed to be mini-shrunken heads on the tips.

Sam introduced her as May the Mighty. Her left shoulder bore the same blue tattoo of a fist as Sam had. She was muscular with a smile that drifted downward at the edges. She filled her share of the booth amply.

"Mom couldn't get enough of the slam-bang game action," said Sam. "She wanted the big guys in the middle of the line to pick up the people across from them, twirl them around, and drop-kick them onto the turf." She explained that May had been part of the professional wrestling circuit and met her father, Ted "Earthquake" Torquemada, that way. He'd died of a heart attack two years ago.

"She was pleased with your last run today. It sort of reminded her of the somersaults and kamikaze spins they'd do in the ring."

I told her I had planned nothing. I just let the moves come instinctively.

"That's the way we did 'em too," said May. "Monkeyshines, we called it."

I could immediately see where Sam got her personality. Her mom still looked quite capable of entering a wrestling ring with theatrical flair.

Sam said she couldn't field all the calls and messages she was handling on my phone and devices under her supervision. "I could say you've left the premises for Disney World, your reward for being named MVP."

"They don't do that for high schoolers, do they?" inquired Ladarius.

"What do Cascadians know? In an age of big-money football, anything goes."

"It's hard to believe that this town, this whole region, was so starved for recognition," said Lad. "I mean, we could've had a president elected from Cascades, an astronaut walk on the moon, a couple win *Dancing with the Stars*, and it wouldn't have gotten the same outpouring of joy that this football team got. We players felt a little of it going in, but at the end it was like a tidal wave carrying every one of us."

"The school, too," said Sam. "You could feel it in the halls, in the classrooms.

Something big was happening that we couldn't exactly put our fingers on. I don't even think Sublimious saw it coming."

"I'm lucky I saw the goal line coming at the end of the game," I confessed.

We had plates of food piled in front of us. Any kind of soft drink we wanted. People kept trying to ply us with alcohol. We told them any kind of hard stuff would probably sink us into a coma.

When Big Nico had a chance to pull me aside, he expressed his thanks "for saving his ass." He said he'd been sweating bullets at the end of the game. He had a couple of big bets on us, and he was getting three points, but we were down by five with seconds left in the game. He shivered. "I could've had co-owners of my restaurant if you hadn't made that last-ditch catch."

I didn't tell him his own son would've disowned him if it had come to that.

Gamer Burke Pennypack swung by the booth. He was upbeat because he felt that he could synchronize my final run-catch into a *Road to Glory* e-sports mode that he might be able to sell to Electronic Arts.

"That company might be thinking of producing a high school version of their college football video game," he said, waving his arms. "I could goose up your final play on the video, have you hurdle a defender backward, stiff-arm a couple barbarians, maybe fly a little like the Vulture or DeathBird. Whaddaya think, Sublim, I could get you part of the action and you can cash in like the college players with their name, image, and likeness?"

I didn't know what he was talking about, but Ladarius and his dad did.

"Do you really think that's what drives Sublimious?" asked Lad. "Becoming part of a video, cashing in on the action?"

Burke boomed, "Hey, if it boosts his brand and leverages his marketing power, I say, 'Go for it!'"

"If it's legal, why not?" added Big Nico.

His son didn't say it, but I knew he thought it: Since when did his dad care about legal?

*　*　*

At about two in the morning, Ladarius hauled me out of the main restaurant, which was still crawling with festive revelers. We had to leave Sam and her mother. May the Mighty had been arm wrestling all comers for the last two hours and defeating them one by one with husky shouts of triumph.

"Gawd, how did you ever hook up with Samantha Schneider?" asked Lad.

"She takes care of my correspondence," I said.

"You mean all that crap that comes over your iPhone and social media?"

"Yes, and it's not all crap. Some of it is very nice and complimentary."

"Man, you are so trusting. You *do* need somebody like Sam screening all that junk. She'll tell them what cliff to jump off if they get annoying."

We retreated to the storage room, which in the last week Lad and his dad had fixed up to be like a small home. They'd brought in a desk, swivel chair, and TV to go along with my cot.

"I finally found your place out by the Gates of Wisdom Forest," Ladarius had told me when they did the renovation. "It was a lousy little rental. But I couldn't find any grandfather."

Lad sat with me, surrounded by shelves and freezers.

"You never did have any parents living with you, even on weekends?" he asked.

"No, but I have a grandfather," I swore.

"He'd better be a guardian, or else you'll be suspended from school, from what I know."

I shrugged. I knew if I said more, it might be incriminating.

"Where are you from?" asked Lad. "You just didn't land here and then started playing football that first day, I'm pretty sure."

I sat in the swivel chair and lay back so that it creaked. "You may not believe this, but that's exactly how it happened."

"But you had to play somewhere before? Some other town or city to be as good as you were when you got here."

Our Powers knew there was always the danger of discovery. They left it up to each explorer to try to explain our origin and presence as best we could.

"I came because I thought Callister Cascades needed a stimulus."

Ladarius was sitting on the edge of the cot. "You're kidding. You were hunting around for a place to land, and you chose our little burg?"

"That's about right. You don't need to know any more, do you?"

"Geez, I don't. But plenty of others might have questions. Like the school administration, coaches, all our opponents."

I breathed deeply. "You're not going to turn me in, are you?"

"Come on, and ruin the greatest Cascades football season in history?"

I leaned forward and held out my hand. "Deal, okay?"

"Sublim, I always knew you were something else."

We shook.

* * *

The Oracles sent a message that the Emissary had watched the championship game from afar. Our Liege didn't understand the play-by-play, but he had the Interpreters define the final outcome. He was pleased that I had made such an indelible impression.

He wished to meet with me in the safe house when all the excitement had died down. The deluge of adulation was another aspect of the American football culture that the Keysians needed to understand. Was this the expectation at the end of every season, or only when your particular team accomplished something extraordinary? What happened to teams and communities whose achievements were ordinary, or to those who, unfortunately, failed?

The Emissary had to be aware that if we embedded individuals as talented as Sublimious Z. Hormats (a.k.a. Clancy), then every Keysian could be judged by the same advanced metrics. Must we send only the best, or can we dispatch common stock or even those below standards?

How was I going to be treated once the football season was over? Would Callister Cascades let me blend back into society? Did the players face other challenges or have other obligations?

I wasn't sure I had the answers. I had more to learn.

I thought seriously about postponing the meeting. Using the excuse that I had to decompress after the game, and the wild atmosphere that took hold of everybody who was so totally invested in the outcome. Ladarius told me the next thing to watch for was a "big head."

That was hard to comprehend.

My head, I knew from looking in mirrors, was already slightly larger than most eleventh-grade students. I kept my brown hair short for sanitary purposes. My eyebrows were arched, my nose aquiline, my mouth taut, my ears smallish and slightly pointed. Back in Keysiana, we had worked on this sculpting to make me appear more proportionate to the average human.

Lad explained that my head would not actually grow visibly. But it could fill with self-importance, vanity and cockiness. I might even "walk taller" and look down on people who hadn't reached the pinnacle that the Rams and I had.

I told him I didn't think I would fall into such a prideful trap. These were pitfalls I had to watch for and tell the Emissary about. Winning and standing out were one thing, but humility and accepting one's limitations were part of football and all sports in America. It was a test of character that I had to learn.

I could tell the Emissary that this process was almost as vital as reaching the top. Would he and the Powers understand this subtlety?

I was frightened my mission might be over and that I would be recalled before I learned everything I had been sent to absorb and pass on. I thought that if I could delay our meeting, I would have more value to convey.

So I sent word that I was tired. The game, the acclamation and the scrutiny had taken everything out of me. I would get in touch after I had time to recover.

16

That Monday when I walked into homeroom, my desk was covered with hundreds of texts and emails that Samantha had printed out from my phone and other devices she kept under my name. The themes were similar: You did the impossible. You made us proud to be from Callister Cascades... to go to this school. I was glad to say that I knew you (although most I'd never met or heard of).

Sam had sifted through all the messages and answered most with what she called a "personal acknowledgment that wasn't very personal."

Some notes had a hint of exasperation: "Why did you guys dig yourselves such a deep hole?" "You didn't have to give us heart failure by waiting until the last play to score." "Now that I've replayed your final run-and-catch on my phone camera, you could've done without the last acrobatics—that was just showing off!"

Sam had also highlighted a few communications from college athletic departments asking if they could send a representative to meet and speak with me. Or if I'd like to visit their campus to see how I might fit into their football program.

"I'm not an expert on the Notre Dames and Georgias of the world, but I understand that if you play football for them, they'll take real good care of you," Sam said. "Like give you a key to the sauna with a lot of naked co-eds."

When I walked the halls, I couldn't navigate through the clusters of classmates who conveyed compliments, gratitude and downright joy for my performance. I high-fived, fist bumped, hugged, and shook hands. Honestly, I was overwhelmed by how much they said I had made their day, week, year… life.

"Geez," I answered, it wasn't only me. "It was Prince, Ladarius, the whole team and coaches who fashioned victory. You can include the cheerleaders and the band and the fans in the stands who stood behind us and gave us the drive to have a great season and win the championship."

Ladarius counseled on how to manage the halls, the crowds, the individual enthusiast. You bow your head, shrug your shoulders, wave away plaudits. "Aw, I was just doing my job," he said to say. Or, "football is a team sport. We needed each player and coach to contribute everything they had."

Lad was really good at "working the crowd," as he termed it. I watched him laugh, deflect compliments, and give credit right down to the locker room attendant who collected the dirty uniforms.

"Sublim, you did as much and probably more than anybody," he said. "But act humble and walk lightly. That way they'll get to know you're a class act."

I was invited to parties by students I didn't even know. Girls proposed we go out on dates or back to their houses, preferably when their parents weren't home. Clubs in school asked me to join. The drama workshop inquired if I wanted to try out for the play *Our Town* to be the stage manager. Downtown businesses offered me part-time and even full-time jobs, or to do testimonials for their products. Nonprofit organizations and charities wondered if I would help them raise funds.

Burke Pennypack asked if I would kick off the e-sports league in the high school's electronics game hall in the new year. "Criminey, you might even be starring in one of the new videos for all we know," he said with his usual zeal.

In a quiet moment with Sam, I asked, "What if I had dropped that last pass from Prince? What if we had been wiped out by Allendale? Would all these folks want to be my best friend?"

"They'd probably want to dump your body in some unmarked grave in the

Gates of Wisdom Forest," she replied candidly. "They'd invite you to their house for a poison dinner. They'd build a straw monument of you on the school steps and shoot arrows at it."

"You didn't have to be so graphic," I said.

"Well, you've got to be aware of the gamut of human passions. If you didn't have me around, you'd be wandering down the yellow brick road and the Wizard would turn you into a tin woodsman."

Sam the Slam and Ladarius instinctively knew my safety was at risk whenever I ventured out on my own. That was why I ducked under their protective umbrella whenever I could. I was like a doe I glimpsed occasionally out on a wooded path in the Gates of Wisdom: I needed to go where the trees were so thick the hunters never looked.

*　　*　　*

As the week of celebration moved on, Mr. Fasciola suggested another lunch in his homeroom. He'd bring pizza and homemade root beer that he saw being sold in a stall at the Amish market.

"So I guess you've been crowned Prince of Callister Cascades," he began.

"Oh, no, sir, Prince is our quarterback. I don't know whether it's his first or last name."

"Are you for real or pulling my leg?"

"If I pulled your leg, you'd know it. Coach Dan has taught me the proper tackling technique so that I'd stop you in your tracks."

"Yeah, but he didn't use you enough on defense."

"He was saving me. He said even jet assists can be subject to entropy."

"Are we talking about the same Dan Kerkegaard I know at this school?"

"Yes, he teaches environmental science, I think."

"I'd venture to guess it's more like woodshop. Not that that's unimportant.

I wanted to know how to make a birdhouse at your age."

Mr. Fasciola liked to eat. He had ordered a Margherita pizza and destroyed the first slice in six bites.

"Have you adjusted to being most popular in Callister Cascades High School, even if 95 percent of the student body doesn't know you from Adam?"

I was sure Mr. Fasciola was exaggerating. He said he wasn't. He was trying to point out the superficiality of human nature. "Most people want to feel good about themselves, and if you help them reach that level of nirvana for an extended moment in their lives, they will be eternally grateful."

I wanted to argue, which is probably what he wanted me to do. He liked debates in his history class.

"I guess you're right," I said as I drank the root beer, which was delicious.

"Sure, I'm right. The masses don't sit back and analyze. Football can be like mainlining instant gratification if your team wins—and wins as big as you did. Who delivered the final denouement? You did, so you're *the man*."

"I didn't do it to be the man, as you say."

"I know that too," Mr. Fasciola said. "You did it because you love the game, and you're so good at it, you just delivered without giving a damn about how it would affect 10,000 other people. And I'm probably underestimating that number."

"You know more about me than I may know about myself."

"Oh, no, I don't think that. I'm just a teacher who likes to theorize." He was plowing into another piece of pizza. "I can't really say what motivates you. I'd venture to guess that you get something out of performing extraordinary feats, and the impact on others is simply a repercussion."

I always liked to hear his theories in class. He thought Eisenhower was a better president than Americans gave him credit for. He argued that if America didn't go into Vietnam, its leaders would have gone into someplace else in the name of stopping communism.

"What do you think comes now?" he asked. "With the season over."

"I can't tell you, I've been concentrating on football for the last half year. I'm not sure where I will direct my energy now that it's done."

Of course, I couldn't tell him the whole truth: That I might be leaving abruptly and going back to Keysiana.

"You like American history. You might read a few books on it. I could recommend *Give Me Liberty* by Eric Foner, *The Oxford History of the American People* by Samuel Eliot Morison, or *Atlas Shrugged* by Ayn Rand. The last one's not really history, but we could really chew over the author's message."

"I appreciate your suggestions," I said, not very enthusiastically.

"I know, you're in high school. It's hard to wean yourself off Instagram."

"Yes, I like to text back and forth," I lied. I pictured Sam making a big googly-eyed face at me.

"What I would tell you, however," said Mr. Fasciola, chowing down on his third pizza slice, "is watch out. You've risen to the top of the heap, you and your championship buddies. There may be a few people who think you've gotten full of yourselves and might want to cut you down to size. Others might want to take advantage of you or convince you to use your status for something that might not be really right for who you are."

"I'm still learning who I am," I answered. "Now that football's done, those lessons might become even a little harder. I didn't realize that when I started."

"If you've got questions as you go along, there's always lunch."

Teaching history must work up an appetite.

*　*　*

I met with the Emissary after an intermediary sent a message that the Master was perturbed that I had delayed our meeting. I could tell the pique by the sounds that came inside the safe house. Sighs that resembled muffled spurts of steam.

Throat clearing bordering on a saw cutting through thick wood.

You are not getting too big for your britches, are you? asked my Liege.

I didn't even know he knew such human vernacular.

"No, sire, I merely wanted to sample some of the reactions of the Callister Cascaders after the big game. You can appreciate that it is part of the feedback loop," I replied.

Yes, I thought you might be susceptible to excessive praise. I feared you might accept that offer to be the stage manager in Our Town. That was one of my favorite plays when Keysiana began to study American literature.

Honestly, the Chieftain was catching me off guard. I didn't realize he was becoming that immersed in the vast repositories of human culture.

"You and the Powers have given me a wide berth to embed in and understand American football. It has been a true learning experience to become such an integral part of this most indispensable of sports. But I am at a point where I must learn more. Like what comes after the season is over. Do the team followers continue the accolades and excesses, or do they move on?"

The next sound I heard was a long, pensive throat clearing.

You are telling the Authorities that you are not ready to return yet?

"I think that is my preference. There is more than the playing, discipline and camaraderie of the regular season. If we are going to fit into this full life, we must understand what happens beyond the locker room. What are the expectations and obligations of a well-rounded athlete to become one of *them*?"

What was unexpected about the Emissary was that He occasionally hit you with a broadside of humor. I heard it coming with a most raffish sound similar to

"Tee-hee... Tee-hee...Tee-hee."

Sublimious, you are not talking about spending time with an American girl, are you? I believe they call it 'shacking up.'

Where that came from, I'll never know. I didn't even have such a phrase in the extensive vocabulary that I had been taught for my visitation.

"Sire, I don't think that is even worthy of my reply."

Well, you don't have to get uppity. We at the doors of the Kingdom must test all motivations of our explorers once they leave the confines of our culture. We have the right to probe even lifestyles that may compromise you in your new environs.

"My heartfelt apologies. American girls have not become a preoccupation, although I'll admit they could be."

He reestablished proper decorum. A refreshing air swept the safe room.

You may remain, Sublimious Z. Hormats, but we always maintain the right to revoke your stay at any moment. Do not abuse this privilege.

17

Ladarius couldn't believe some of the invitations he received from college football programs shortly after the season was over. He was a rising senior. He had been debating whether to go to a local community college or to a technical academy to learn a trade. He wasn't even thinking about playing in college. However, the state championship had changed all that.

When a large university known for its nationally ranked football schedule contacted him and asked if he'd like to visit, tour its campus and facilities and meet some of the coaches, he thought, *Why not?*

The recruiter also said, "Why don't you bring along that super-fast team-mate of yours. The gawky kid who only started playing this year."

Ladarius told the recruiter he'd ask.

"Hey, Sublim, you've got to go. They said all-expenses paid."

The assistant head coach met us at the all-glass athletic center, which was larger than the administration building and the president's office combined.

"Yo, what do you expect?" said our welcomer. "Our head coach has a bigger salary and a longer contract than the president."

The guide's name was Ben Outland. He said we could call him "Bruiser." He was one of six assistant head coaches. "Coaching inflation, sorta like grade inflation," he laughed. "I'm in charge of bribing guys off the transfer portal, lining up big donors to pay players, and showing all you turkeys around our facilities."

We didn't know whether to take Bruiser seriously or not. It seemed like he had done this so many times before that he was bored by the whole routine.

"You guys played at some little half-ass school that won a state champion-ship, didn't you?" he said. "Our head coach, Popeye Lloyd, told me, 'Show 'em around. We need some normal small-time players to mix with our five-star prima donnas who got big heads and big bank accounts.'"

Ladarius and I looked at each other. It seemed like we were familiar with that phrase, "big heads." We had measured ours and concluded they weren't.

Bruiser walked fast and spewed out facts about the super-facilities we were touring. "Locker rooms change colors to match the players' moods... Ferrari leather chairs so big-boy asses don't get any blisters... Marble shower rooms, barbershops, Jacuzzis, massage rooms, hyperbaric chambers, nutrition stations, arcade game rooms, and separate sleeping pods for each player.

"We make sure our student-athletes are pampered like they should be. They present the university's face to the public after all. If our quarterback's gonna be a number one draft choice, that's how a lot of people see us. If we go twelve and two and do well in the end-of-year playoffs, then we've done our jobs to keep the school on the side of the angels."

Ladarius inquired about class requirements for football players.

"We don't push 'em. Six credits during fall semester is all our boys have to carry. Some put more on their plate. Depends on how committed they are to their future profession. If it's football, we want them concentratin' on that and little else."

Ladarius shrugged. "Seems like it might take forever to graduate if you only take six credits each semester."

"Hey, we want 'em focused on what they're here for during the season," said Bruiser. "And that's blocking and tackling. They got the rest of the year to take business relations or contract law or whatever else they think will help them down the road in their lives."

Ladarius laughed. "Well, Bruiser, at least you're honest."

"Sure, man, I'm not about to lead you astray. You come here to put your bodies on the line for Big Blue. *Then* you worry about your future."

As we walked down what seemed like miles of hallways with huge photos of great players from yesteryear and the recent past, Bruiser led us into a beautiful room with soft couches, big screens and soothing music.

"This is our NIL meeting room. You know what that stands for, right? Name, image, and likeness. Potential sponsors or rich alums come in here, meet with the blue-chippers, and work out deals to pay them. Hey, endorse a Michelin tire and get a couple thou . . . Claim you eat Mrs. Sanchez's chicken enchiladas, you get an ad on Facebook and all the Tex-Mex you can chow down on.

"We don't care what kind of hookup you work out, long as it passes a board of examiners. You can sit on the hood of a pickup for sale, invite the homeless to a soup kitchen, or walk the streets with a sandwich board urging a vote for the mayor. We don't even mind if you kick back a little to the university athletic fund. It's a free country."

"Let's say I come here," said Ladarius. "Nobody's ever heard of me. Am I going to have as much of a shot at the NIL or the share-the-pot money as a star quarterback?"

Bruiser smiled. "What do you think? You can maybe endorse a shoelace."

Ladarius was staring at a painting of the university's Heisman Trophy candidate unleashing a perfect pass. "What about an offensive guard who keeps your star quarterback from getting sacked? Is he going to get an endorsement?"

"Well, maybe not. But the pretty boy can kick some of his own money to him. We find our ace players will share a little, especially if a guy in the trenches is keeping a big bear from ripping up the QB's MCL."

Bruiser liked telling us about some of the NIL deals he was involved in with his players. Like the school's star running back was doing TV ads for the local Mercedes-Benz dealer and given a bright red C-Class Cabriolet to drive around campus, the dealer even recruited co-eds to ride with him in the front seat. Or how the Samoan defensive lineman got to host a luau with a genuine fire-knife dance sponsored by a big grocery chain.

"I mean, this is stuff our players couldn't even dream about a few years ago."

When the coach took us into the team's weight and strength-training gym, our eyes could barely take in all the racks, benches, and machines. They glistened a polished black and silver.

He then turned to me and said, "We got a report you ran the 40 in 3.9 seconds. First of all, nobody runs it that fast, so we think the podunks at your school were cheatin'. You come here, we'll time you right and develop your speed to the absolute max."

"Mr. Bruiser," I said, "I can assure you I run it that fast. Maybe faster."

"Sure, kid, sure," he waved me off. "We had a d-back who ran a 4.2. People in the know told me we goosed the time up for him so he could get drafted in the NFL's first round."

When we finally got back to where we had started, Bruiser asked us what we thought of the vast, dedicated athletic facilities.

"Your place is really something," said Ladarius. "It reminds me of a movie with the best computer-generated imagery. Every room I entered felt like I was on the deck of *Starship Troopers*."

Bruiser didn't know what to make of that, and neither did I.

I thanked him for the invitation and the tour. "You know," I said. "I can't believe all this is just concentrated on football. I mean, you should have at least one room devoted to American history with stacks of books and blown-up photos of FDR, Albert Einstein and Neil Armstrong. Players could sit in pods and listen to the story of the Spanish-American War."

"Yeah, well, we got places where they can listen to Drake and Tyler, The Creator."

"I'm sure they're historical in their own way," I said.

I concluded by shaking Bruiser's hand and saying, "I have been living in a storage room beneath a Greek restaurant. I'm not sure I could get used to this luxury, but the pampering for those who perform is very nice. It's not quite clear what you do with the others who don't live up to expectations."

"We ask 'em to take up an academic life."

* * *

When I returned to school, Sam informed me that I had been selected to the All-State football team. "That means somebody thinks you were one of the twenty-five best players in our state this year," she explained. "You get to go to a banquet in the state capitol with the governor and the other honorees. You also get to take a guest. Why don't you take me?"

"What do I do? Do I have to make a speech or anything?"

"No, you just have to dress up. Maybe wear a tux and have a beautiful girl on your arm. In your case, you can come with a tough, tattooed hard case."

"You always dismiss yourself," I said. "I will be proud to take you since you are smart and you're what they call my, ah, publicist."

All the other Cascades wide receivers congratulated me on the honor. I confided to Ladarius, "Deep down, I suspect you're envious and maybe more than a little angry. Here I come along and in a year I'm receiving the tributes you think are rightfully yours."

Lad shrugged. "Yeah, that might be in the back of a few minds. But we know that without you, we wouldn't have been nearly as good. We wouldn't have gone to State and wouldn't be getting the praise we're getting. Even girls who'd never look at us before now are more interested."

"Geez, as long as you put it in that context, I guess you owe me."

Ladarius was always straight with me. I had been made aware of jealousy, stealing acclaim from others, and arriving from seemingly nowhere and eclipsing reputations that had been built over years. The Emissary and Oracles had warned me. So had Lad with his rules of the road and playing within the confines of the game. I had strived to stay modest, not stick out like the exposed nail, but sometimes my inherent Keysian gifts had broken free. I couldn't help it.

I asked Lad if there was something I could do for my brothers before I went to the All-State banquet to acknowledge that they had helped me reach that special status.

"You worry too much. Take it in stride. All of us are happy for you."

Of course, I had more on my mind than just being a responsible and appreciative brother. I was concerned about the revelation of who I was and why I was here. I had to find ways to protect my identity and purpose.

"How about if I buy them each a bracelet with 'Ragin' Receivers' on it?"

"That sounds hokey," said Ladarius.

"I am only original on the field," I admitted. "I'm a little dull as a regular citizen."

"Ah, hang," he finally said. "Why don't we have our own banquet at Drakos? Doesn't have to be a big deal. Dad gets to whip up something special for us. He'd like that, and you could say your own thanks in any way you want."

We settled on that kind of arrangement. Then Lad gave me a crooked smile. "You're actually taking Samantha Schneider to the All-State banquet?"

"What's wrong with that?" I said. "I'm sure she'll make an impression."

"Oh, that she will."

* * *

On a Friday night, without school the next day, Ladarius convinced all six wide receivers and our quarterback, Prince, to join him and me at Drakos. He sold it as a celebration of "the hands and arms" brigade that made Callister Cascades the football team of the year.

"We're a special fraternity that reached above and beyond expectations," he told everybody. "We'll get together and tell a few lies about ourselves and see if we can understand in our own small ways how we did what we did."

Big Nico put us in a back room. He brought out one course after another. He described them as he placed each before us. He didn't say it, but I knew he'd made enough money on his championship game bets that he could feed us like kings. The secret stayed between us. I knew his son despised his gambling on anything, but especially on our team.

All of us receivers had practiced together, played tough games together, healed together in the treatment room and whirlpool, and listened to coaches together before games. Yet we really didn't know each other deep down. So as we ate, Ladarius made each player stand up and briefly say something, anything, about himself that none of us might know.

Aurelius said his name was of Latin origin, meaning golden or gilded. It was also the name of a second-century Roman emperor. His father didn't know any of this until he looked it up on the night he was born. His mother was very religious and wanted to call him Ezekiel. His father refused to name any kid of his Ezekiel because he'd probably end up being called Zeke.

He jabbed me as he told his story. "Come to think of it, Sublimious, you're sort of golden. Why didn't your old man call you Aurelius?"

"He knew we already had one on the team," I answered. I felt it was a pretty clever response when I knew I wasn't really clever.

Styles told us his last name was Johnson. Still, they called him Styles on the stadium PA system whenever he made a reception. His father was a sanitary engineer, or trashman. His three older sisters played field hockey, basketball, and lacrosse, and pushed him to play sports. Styles was going on a grant-in-aid to play at a historic black college where the coach projected him to be a steady go-to receiver.

Heath Jensen, our only white starter, was born with spondylosis, which is a curvature of the spine, and had an operation when he was young to straighten it. He developed great hands since he knew he was slow. Heath received offers to play at a small college, but wanted to study finance and be an accountant. He also had designs on marrying his steady girlfriend. Overall, he confessed his life was dull and planned.

Kadeem, last name Nabors, was a gymnast as well as a football wide receiver. He told us he might have an opportunity to do both in college, thanks to his single mother, who worked two jobs. Kadeem confessed that he resented me at first because I stole his playing time. Then he saw how I made the team more successful and a vital part of the school. He liked being part of something larger than himself.

Bottoms, first name Terrence, was only a sophomore, yet was a student of the game, ran precise pass routes, and studied films of the great receivers: Jerry Rice, Marvin Harrison and Larry Fitzgerald. His father was a postman, his mother was a hairdresser, and his two younger brothers were already taller than him. Bottoms's family had a pet Aussie Shepherd, and he had taught him to catch Frisbees just as consistently as he caught passes.

Murphy, nicknamed "Biggens," had problems with the law, truancy, and run-ins with coaches. His father was often a no-show, while an older brother was a cryptocurrency dealer who lived in a mansion. Murphy hoped to be a "big man" like his brother. He resented that he wasn't a starter, which made his concentration ebb at times.

Prince said he knew he was invited because the receivers couldn't live without him. He'd been a three-year starter and practiced hard, so he'd be "clutch" in big moments. Prince said he appreciated me because my speed and hands made him look good. He received several offers from medium-sized colleges with a chance to start as a freshman. However, he refused to disclose whether Prince was his first or last name.

Ladarius asserted that he was the leader, captain, organizer, and philosopher of the wide receivers because it came naturally. The rest of us all booed. Torn between playing in college or going to a trade school, Lad said he might toss a coin to choose between the two.

"Why don't you learn to cook and join your father in Drakos?" someone asked. Lad replied that he didn't think they could co-exist next to each other all day.

In truth, I think the brothers were all waiting to hear me reveal some of my personal secrets. I had thought about this ever since Lad first told me about his idea.

"I always wanted to play football from an early age," I began. "But we moved around a lot. So I studied the game from afar, and then when I got my chance this year, I took it. You guys and the coaches showed me all the football fundamentals and techniques. I just applied them."

Most of the crew groaned. "Yo, you can't drill speed!" hollered Aurelius.

"Comes naturally." I tried to brush the comment off.

"Don't give us that. Usain Bolt got natural speed, and you don't look nothin' like Usain Bolt."

"Well, would you rather I didn't show it?" I said, not belligerently.

"Oh, you can show it, baby. We just wondered how you oiled them camshafts."

Ladarius intervened. He was great at saving the day.

"It was really Sublimious's idea to have this little get-together. He actually didn't want to go off to the All-State shindig without expressing his thanks to all of us for helping him reach that honor. He knows that without Prince throwing, and all of us opening up gaps and seams for him to run to, he wouldn't have made it."

"Yeah, man, we know he 'preciates us," said Styles. "How could he not? We gotta be out on the field for him and Prince to work their stuff. Sometimes, though, we get a little annoyed when the coaches zero in and huddle up with him, and only him. They put so much trust in Sub, we feel like we're extra spokes to the wheel."

"He couldn't help it if Dan or Sawyer designed a special play around him," answered Ladarius. "He has the ability to break a game open, so they went with him at critical times."

"Yeah, gotcha. It's just why can't it be me and the other guys disappearing in the rearview mirror every now and then?"

I sensed they probably wanted more. I didn't need Ladarius to keep defending me, so I jumped in. "When I get back from the All-State gathering," I said, "I'd like to do one more thing with all of you before most of you graduate and go your separate ways. I don't know what it is yet, but let's all think on it. We can't just say 'that's it.' We've got to find some way to remember how special this championship was."

When everyone left and I helped Ladarius and his dad clean up, Lad said, "I'm glad you said what you did at the end. There seems to still be a little mending to do, and we all should think on what that might be."

"Good," I laughed. "You are the brains behind us, whether anybody wants to admit it or not."

"Oh, I don't know." Lad shrugged. "Sometimes brains are overrated."

18

SAMANTHA TOOK ME TO GET FITTED FOR A RENTAL TUXEDO FOR THE All-State banquet. I looked like what Aurelius would call "a dick." Tall and gawky to begin with, I stood rod-straight with a white shirt collar jutting out like flippers from the neck and a long jacket that made me look like an Antarctic penguin.

Sam said her mother, May the Mighty, had taken her to pick out a dress. She had gone to a store most WWE wrestlers frequented for special occasions. I feared it might be a whip and spurs.

The sponsors of the event actually sent a sleek black limousine to take us on the three-hour trip to the state capitol. Sam wore a heavy full-length khaki Army coat, so I couldn't see what she had on underneath. She also had a watch cap covering her head. But I could see her shoes, and they frightened me. They were open-toed with thick four-inch-high heels, apparently made for stomping bad guys in street alleys.

Sam saw me looking at them and said, "Don't worry, my dress is very tasteful."

I was nervous. Sam had done her research on the other high school players who were elected to the All-State team. One was Jake Paretsky, the quarterback for Allendale, whom we'd beaten in the championship. He probably wouldn't be happy to see me. Others were All-Americans and five-star recruits who were going to universities like Michigan, Iowa, Miami, Georgia, Clemson, and Penn State upon graduating.

"Do I even belong in the same room with these guys?" I asked.

"Hey, you belong if somebody says you belong."

Sam was chewing gum and popping bubbles. She always seemed comfortable in her own skin, which may have perturbed many of our schoolmates. They had labeled her a bull dyke, butch, Celtic queen, tranny, and drag mother. I didn't care what they called her. She had befriended me that first day, and we'd only grown closer.

During the football season, she had handled all my social contacts. "You don't need these dumbfries calling and texting, and sending you nude photos of themselves. I'll handle them and make you seem cool at the same time."

Ladarius was always skeptical. "Doesn't she want anything from you?" he'd ask. "Money, sex, a rep by hanging with a jock?"

"I don't think so," I said. "She just likes me 'cause I like her. Everybody else dumps on her without knowing the least thing about her."

So Sam rode with me in the back seat of a limo, tilting a bottle of ginger ale to her lips, then spreading her arms wide across the cushioned seats like we were going to a picnic. "Sublimious, did you ever think we'd be riding in luxury that first day we met in Mr. Fasciola's homeroom?"

"Sam, I barely knew where I was that day."

We reached the site of the banquet, a swank downtown hotel in the center of the capitol. We walked up the steps past a footman in a top hat. He bowed and said, "Good evening, ma'am. Good evening, sir."

Sam led us to the coat-check cubicle. When she removed her Army coat, my jaw dropped. Her shoulders and neck were bare. Her breasts were covered by a black halter top with iridescent blue flowers placed strategically where they needed to be. A black mini dress dotted with stars and swirling planets ran from her hips to just above her knees. Filmy black strips of fringe swayed off it to her ankles. Her midriff was proudly bare. Her muscled legs were visible above the knees.

"WHOA, KILLER MAMA!!!"

I thought perhaps I said it, but I didn't have any such phrase in my vocabulary.

It was a tall, handsome young man behind me. Probably one of the All-Staters.

Sam's face was tastefully rouged and lipsticked. Her hair wasn't the blonde bowl it usually was. It was brushed up and back; strands fell artfully over her eyes.

"Geez, Sam, you look... You look... spectacular."

I hadn't even seen the black rose tattoo she had flowing from her elbow to her upper right shoulder. It complemented the smaller blue fist on her left bicep.

As we walked into the vast dining auditorium, every eye turned toward her. I almost burst out with a "Thank you, thank you" because they weren't watching me. They couldn't. Sam had stolen the show. If Mr. Fasciola's homeroom, if nine-tenths of Callister Cascades' student body could have seen her, they'd have let out a collective gasp, and exclaimed, "Where have you been hiding?!"

We sat at tables of eight. There was an elevated dais up front with seats for the governor and other dignitaries. The whole setup was very elegant. Waiters in tails and waitresses in white gowns filled water goblets, took drink orders (non-alcoholic), and passed around hors d'oeuvres.

At our table was a huge defensive tackle headed for Notre Dame; he made sure we knew that right away. He had brought his mother. Two other All-Staters, normal-sized and oozing confidence, had brought dates. None was as striking as Sam. Compared to her, they were just ordinary down-home girls with fluffy corsages and extravagant shocks of brown hair draping their shoulders.

I could see my counterparts slipping mesmerized glimpses at Sam, especially when she leaned forward and the tops of her breasts crested from her halter. "So, are all of you guys going to get part-time jobs your first year at college?" she asked in her usual teasing tone of voice.

They stared at her as if she were some wild goose who had flown in and landed on their pond. But it broke the ice. They all started talking freely about where they came from, what they thought about being named All-State, and how they imagined their first year of college football might go.

Sam had that effect on people. She came right at them. There was a reason why she was called Sam the Slam. She "slammed" into those she met. At school, many saw her as obnoxious, conceited, a "bull in a china shop," as some put it. But here at the banquet table, she was just a bold conversation-starter.

"Did any of you guys growing up think you'd be one of the most outstanding football players in the state?" she asked.

"My father had me throwing a football before I could walk," one joked.

Another said, "My coach told me every day I could get better."

"What about you, Sub-lum?" A player was trying to read my name tag.

I had to admit I was a little intimidated by these super-physical specimens. "I—I had to study the game a long time before I decided to play."

"What's to study?" the player going to Notre Dame said. "They put you in a barrel, you fight bears and king cobras, and whoever comes out the other end wins."

Sam interjected, "Yeah, but what Sublimious found was that he could run away from all those frightening beasts. He was faster than any of them."

One of the girl companions turned to Sam. "You help him with his studying? I'd say you might be somewhat of a distraction."

"Oh, no." Sam gave her a hard stare. "Sublimious doesn't distract. I take care of anything that might interfere with his concentration."

"I'll bet," the companion said edgily.

The banquet proceeded through walnut salads, prime roast beef, and cherries jubilee. Then speeches by a famous NFL coach and the governor, who lauded us All-Staters as not only the best in the state but the best in the nation because of the football excellence our state had cultivated for decades.

Each honoree then had his picture and his achievements projected up on a screen the size of a Jumbotron. Mine read: Sublimious Z. Clancy, wide receiver-defensive back-kick returner, Callister Cascades High School, Class A State Champions, 56 pass receptions for 972 yards, 17.7 yards per catch, scored winning touchdowns in three games, including state championship.

Jake Paretsky groaned from an adjacent table when he read that last citation.

At the end of a long night of accolades and highlights, many attendees came up and shook my hand, but I could see them eyeing Sam. Even the governor shook my hand and then quickly turned to Sam and crooned, "And whom might this delightful young lady be?"

Sam grabbed his hand and pumped it mightily. "Sam Schneider, running cover for my friend Sublimious Clancy. We're both glad you could extend him this honor. It will look good on his résumé."

The governor stepped back. "You sound like his promoter."

"You know it, Gov. He's star quality."

As we rode back in the limo, I almost fell asleep and dreamed that Sam was as slam-bang beautiful as she had been throughout this night. My dreams were answered when Sam surprisingly leaned in and tilted her head so that her lips were almost touching mine.

"Feel free to kiss me," she whispered. "You know, there were a lot of guys there tonight who wanted to do more than just kiss me."

I tilted forward and began to kiss her chastely. Sam then reached over with her rose-tattooed arm, grasped the back of my head, yanked me in tight, and really gave me an open-mouth kiss to remember.

It lasted a good, firm minute and tasted like a cherry Tootsie Pop dipped in a brain-swirling sweet liquor. I thought I'd once sampled one at the 7-Eleven.

"Geez, Sam," I said when I came up for air. "You were amazing tonight."

"You know it, babes. Now I go back to being a prickly horned toad."

"Not in my eyes. I will remember you this gorgeous and gossipy forever."

* * *

The month after the championship game, after Sam and I had traveled to the All-State banquet, at the start of the new year, Callister Cascades was still basking in the glory of unexpected victory. Banners hung in the school's halls hailing us as STATE CHAMPIONS. In the cafeteria, a banner above the serving stations proclaimed FOOTBALL'S BEST PLAYERS EAT HERE. Before the start of every school day, while we were still in homeroom, one of our players was interviewed for five minutes over the high-tech PA system and got to tell all of his classmates how it felt to be a member of the team that won it all.

Even linemen like Stew Shavers and assistant coaches Tarzan Sampson and Demon Dan Kerkegaard were asked by the host what it was like to suddenly be part of the best team in the state.

Dan proclaimed, "We got to coach a bunch of underachievers who came together and implemented our brilliant game plans and just flat-out beat teams we weren't supposed to beat."

Only a few of us got a chuckle out of his "brilliant game plan" reference. Dan wasn't really that self-promoting, but he did like to plant zingers in the midst of his stream-of-consciousness that mainly his players would pick up on.

Gamer Burke Pennypack asked me one afternoon to join him in the school's e-sports viewing hall. He wanted to show me a new electronic football game just released by Electronic Arts, on which he had been consulted. He said I would be "very, very interested in the realism with which thousands of achievers and killers would soon be playing." I guess "achievers" and "killers" were how some of the gamesters categorized their special playing skills.

For the first time, the company had released a series called *High School Football All-Stars*. I, Sublimious Clancy, was going to be featured in the game-play action. In *All 22+*, which highlights the importance of individual players and their unique abilities, my game-breaking speed, acrobatics, and unpredictable exploits would be available to each e-sports techie.

"There's even a mode where you execute full-body yo-yos around the goalpost crossbar like you did in the New Cambria game," Burke said enthusiastically. "Our players will be really excited to pull up that image and add their own wizardry."

Burke showed me all the animated action projected on the IMAX-sized screen. My image was not the only one shown, but I was recognizable. When the package was released nationwide, I was to get a share of the name, image, and likeness money that each featured player would receive. Since we were still in high school, the NIL money would be placed in escrow until we graduated.

Burke Pennypack sat back, arms folded, looking very self-satisfied. "So, man, what do you think? I got a Callister Cascader into a new presentation that gamers will be playing across the US of A, maybe the whole wide world."

I had always been counseled by my Keysian advisers to be composed, not to let outward emotion instantly seize me like many Americans tend to do. But this time was different.

"Burke, why do you think I play football?" I asked. "Do you think it's so I can turn into some animated cartoon streamed on a screen doing outrageous stunts?"

Burke went rigid in his chair. His hair, which had been flopped over on his cranium, suddenly jacked straight up. "I—I thought you'd be pleased."

"Well, I'm not," I said quietly. "I came here to play and learn what really makes the game special. Not to have a manipulated image doing nip-tucks and crossbar flips. That's for you and your buddies to engineer, but I don't want you putting me in your equation."

Burke's eyes were downcast. "Why did you do those acrobatics then? I thought you were miming a new way of playing, and we gamesters saw it as pure art. We thought, what the blazes, we gotta use that. It's perfect for our purposes."

"I know. I'm not blaming you. It's all the off-the-wall, inconsequential stuff that swirls around football. It might be important to you and your gamesters, but it's wasted air to those of us who play for a deeper reason."

Burke stood up and turned off his console. "I'm sorry you don't approve, but I'm not taking your image back. I love the Sublimious character up on that screen. He can do anything, like you. He may not be real, but boy does he capture our imaginations."

I was sorry for my outburst almost as soon as it happened. It was deliberately rude, and I had been coached to never show any kind of arrogance, a human emotion that the Keysian hierarchy disdained.

Burke, however, was doing what he did best, and what gave him meaning.

The next day, when I saw him in homeroom, I apologized. I should have recognized that he was into his own form of competition as I was on the playing field. I told him he could use my image any way he chose to, but I did not want any form of compensation for lending my name to the project.

He was still a little upset at my impassioned rejection. "You know," he said, "it can get you a national profile. Nobody's heard of Callister Cascades or Sublimious Clancy, but with *High School All-Stars*, it'll put us and you on the map."

I nodded. "Yes, I think I understand its scope and how many gamesters will play it. But I've only been here a year, you see. I'm not Ladarius or Aurelius or Styles. I don't really deserve such attention. They've been doing it far longer."

"Trouble is," said Burke, "they don't have the charisma, the zing. You do. That's what we gamers want. Something to blow the joysticks out of our hands."

"You might incorporate some sort of electrical shock then. Make your gamers' hair stand on end like yours."

PART FOUR

Decision

19

LADARIUS AND HIS DAD HELPED ME FIND A NEW AND BETTER PLACE TO stay with my alleged grandfather. It was a large loft above a garage that belonged to a family they knew who rented it out. It had been fixed up into a comfortable living space. I was told that I couldn't continue staying in the Drakos restaurant storage room.

"It's getting too tight for our distributors to stock our shelves and work around your living arrangement," Big Nico told me. "Besides," he said, "you're starting to smell like a Greek kitchen. We love such fragrance, but when you go out in public, you may become too pungent."

Ladarius also knew I had to be careful to keep the fact that I really had no parents to speak of. He and his father were suspicious of any grandfather-caretaker, but they weren't about to say anything.

Every so often, their curiosity got the best of them. They'd ask, "How did you get here? Where did you come from? Why did you choose to live in Callister Cascades?"

"You could've gone to some big or even medium-sized city," said Lad, "or that prep academy in Florida that develops super athletes."

I always found a way to talk around their inquiries. I'd praise the community for its open-mindedness and receptivity. I'd flatter Ladarius and his dad for their tolerance and broad-mindedness, for being the real caretakers I could depend on who gave a young man a chance to reach his peak. Besides, I'd help make Big

Nico some money on the bets he put down on our team beating the favorites. He'd boast in private about reeling in "suckers" who underestimated our team's growing strength by playoff time.

"You've seen my ability to learn and listen," I'd tell Lad. "You showed me how to fit in, and I'm indebted to you. You had a big hand in making our team an unstoppable force."

I had been taught about appealing to human self-esteem and honor. Even the smartest could be convinced into "going along" if there was something in it for them. My Keysian tutors were very tuned in to the price that friendship could be converted into my goals of embedding and harmonizing.

I didn't think of myself as a "user" or that I was taking advantage of people who were my guides. I knew I was one of many explorers who were probing different aspects of American civilization. Football was but one slice of the complex lifestyle that pulled us like a magnet to small communities, big businesses or influential government agencies. All in all, I had to examine the special culture I was assigned and learn all about it—the good, the bad, the temptations, ego trips, camaraderie, and the price one had to pay for being different.

Sam told me of the community group chats and message boards in which I was mentioned. Classmates, townies, and people from around the state and even the country who had heard about our team's "rise from nowhere," flooded my social media portals with advice, praise, criticisms and offers. "Total strangers feel it is their right to reach out to you to tell you what you should do next or how you might use your talents beyond football," she informed me.

"Do you think I should spend time answering the ones who are trying to be helpful?" I asked.

"I'd say 98 percent of the contacts are from people you don't even know. In fact, you shouldn't even want to know them."

"What are they saying? What if somebody comes up to me in the hall or the lunchroom and asks why I'm not doing what they suggested?"

Sam had returned to her cantankerous self at school. None of her classmates had seen the glamorous, outgoing Samantha Schneider that I had seen at the All-State banquet. They would've sworn it was an impostor. Now she had willingly gone back to becoming my tough, contact-clearing arbiter.

"They want you to come to their parties, meet their sisters, endorse sneakers or Cascades shirts, run in marathons, find inner peace in yoga, speak at their sports clinics, accept gifted pets, help them study for an algebra test, come to dinner and meet their parents, attend bat mitzvahs, and sign autographs at sports bars."

"Do they ever want to discuss American history with me?"

Sam gave me a wink. "For some reason that's never been proposed."

* * *

"Do you know that certain downtown shops are now offering foot-high action figures of a player who looks suspiciously like you?" said Sam. "It's wearing a Callister Cascades blue and gold uniform and a helmet with ram horns. It's reaching out with one hand to catch a football, and at the base, it reads STATE CHAMPS.

"Are you sure it doesn't look like Aurelius or Styles or even Ladarius?" I asked.

"No, I'm pretty sure it's you. The face even replicates your golden hue."

"Oh, geez, I'm going to get in trouble with my brotherhood. They'll think that I'm 'big-timing' them again."

"Well, it's not your fault. It wasn't your idea. But I've even heard that they're giving them away with Wawa hoagies and McDonald's Chicken McNuggets."

"Sam, how's that work? Shouldn't they have asked my permission?"

"I'm no lawyer. But I think if they claim it's only an anonymous Cascades player and not you specifically, then they're just honoring the entire team."

These were the kinds of snags and sinkholes I'd encountered since the end of football. I'd confided to Mr. Fasciola that I found them bewildering. He simply said it came with the territory. I'd have to adapt like I did on the field.

"In that open hundred yards, I could see trouble coming. I'd bob and weave."

"So now you juke mentally. You'll figure it out."

I knew, however, I needed help with the unexpected buffeting from all angles. Sam, as my adviser, always made herself available.

"Look," she said sharply, "many people overstep their bounds. They're trying to show their gratitude for what you did to make them feel good about themselves. They don't know, maybe don't even care, that they're interfering with your life."

I shrugged. "I guess I'd like to say thank you to them all at once and get it over with. Then maybe they'd be satisfied and not ask so much."

"Sorry, Sublim, that's not how it works. Too many want to see something from you beyond the great catch or the last-minute touchdown. They want to know that you're really one of us."

"That's where I rely on you. You have to show me the way."

So Sam proposed an idea. She said that there was a school fair coming up to fund community charities. "It'll have all sorts of things that people can take part in to help raise money for good causes like the SPCA, the senior center, the food pantry. And I'm going to volunteer you for the dunk tank."

"Oh, that sounds painful."

"You don't have to do anything extraordinary. You just sit on a seat above a pool of water, and people pay to throw a ball at a target. If they hit it, the seat releases, and you're dumped into the water. Everyone will get a charge out of seeing their favorite wide receiver drop unceremoniously into the drink."

"Geez, Sam, I can't swim!"

"The water will only be up to your waist at most. It might even be heated."

"I dunno. Being out on a big football field is one thing. However, in this dunk tank, they'll see me up close, and they'll see fear in my eyes."

"My God, Sublimious, you worry too much. All you have to do is sit there in swim trunks and a T-shirt and have a little fun with people who've never seen you in the flesh. It'll make you more human and accessible to them."

I flinched, of course. Sam didn't know—nobody could—that I was Keysian and not *Homo sapien*. Could it be that when they'd see me all wet and scuffling, that I'd change? My golden hue might suddenly alter, and they'd see me for what I was, and I'd lose all control.

"Sam, it's a risk. Yet I'm willing to take it because of you. But if you see me melting or becoming a total fool, you must promise to rescue me."

She promised. Yet for some reason, I pictured her crossing her fingers behind her back or whatever humans do to cancel out a promise.

* * *

On the day of the Callister Cascades School District Fair, I couldn't believe how sprawling the whole event was. Food booths, silent auctions, raffles, pie-eating contests, prize wheels, face painting, a rock-climbing wall, cornhole, cake walks, hoop shoots, bake-offs and chili cook-offs, crafts and painting displays, and petting zoos.

And there I was sitting in a protective cage, on a plastic seat that could be promptly tipped forward into a large basin of water, when a contestant tossed a tennis ball at the center of a target. Clad in only a Rams T-shirt and swim trunks, thankfully, Sam had made sure it was heated for me.

At the top of the cage, a hand-printed sign read: DUNK THE STATE CHAMPS!

Each participant got three tennis balls for two dollars to toss at a circular target, and if one went through an open hole in the center, an electronic mechanism would be triggered, my seat would tilt, and I'd plunge into the pool. Sometimes I wore a snorkel just for laughs.

I took turns with Prince and our running back, Junius Jones. I was by far the most popular in the "chair of no return" because students and townies wanted to know if this Sublimious Z. Clancy was for real. They'd seen him in a uniform, accepting trophies on stages, walking the school halls, eating at the Drakos, even in a painting some student-artist had brushed on a wall. But did he smile or grimace when he was dumped? Did he joke around and seem like one of them? Was it a kick to be superior to the jock who couldn't stop you from humbling him?

At first, I glanced sheepishly at people. They seemed to be licking their chops to drop me into the drink. "Sink the Sublimious!" a few of them chanted. Sam was standing in the crowd, egging them on. "Dump the big deal on his ass! Show him who makes things go round!"

I'd look over and gesture, *What are you doing, Sam? You got me into this. It isn't supposed to be punishment, is it?*

Then the posse, the receivers brotherhood, appeared, and I knew I was in for it. "Hey, Sub baby," Kadeem laughed, "folks seem to got you where they want you—hangin' over the edge of the cliff like you always kept 'em till the last minute."

Styles reared back and fired a ball at the target like it was an arrow between my eyes. "Whew, that felt good!" he roared. "Cool off the boy with the hot hands and jet feet. None of the enemy could. Now I got my shot!"

All the others leaned in, waved their hands, wagged their tongues.

I looked over and saw Sam nodding her head. *Come on, Sub*, she seemed to be saying, *go along. Have some fun. Show them that you can mix it up.*

I climbed out of the water, shook myself like a retriever dog, and suddenly I relaxed. They weren't being intentionally mean. They just jibed and jived like they did on the practice field. I'd learned to take it then; why not now?

I called to Styles, "Looks like you had to buy a dozen balls before you hit the target!"

When Heath stepped up to take a shot, I ragged him, "Hey, here's the only guy who looks gawkier than me. You'll probably miss the target altogether."

My joking with them seemed to recreate the bond that had slowly developed during the season. I'd never really given it to them as hard as they'd given it to me. I always thought they saw me as the coach's ace whom they turned to at crunch time. Now they had a chance to get even, to be more than equal.

Prince was with them. He went into a big, elaborate windup and fired a ball not at the target but at me sitting in the cage. "Man, couldn't help myself," he chuckled. "We always made a direct connection at exactly the right time, didn't we? Wanted to see if you still have good hands even when they're soggy."

I caught the furry ball and threw it back. "Never dropped one, did I?"

"Just checking. Seein' if that winning play wasn't a dream."

The last of our brethren stepped forward, Ladarius. "Yo, Sublim, rules of the road, right? Never stick out like a rusty nail. Well, now you're stickin' out like a hotshot. I'm gonna whack you down to the drowned rat you should be."

Lad chucked the ball right through the center hole, and I fell into the body of water with the loudest splash of the afternoon. He knew what he was doing. He was pounding home that I might have been better than any of them on the field, but I wasn't better anywhere else. The rest didn't know exactly what he was doing. But I did when I thought about it later.

Ladarius always knew how to do exactly the right thing.

The wide receivers wandered off, taunting me over their shoulders. "Man, hope you don't drown, doggie. You don't look like much of a swimmer, jus' like you never looked like much of a pass catcher, till we got proved wrong."

I must have spent three hours in the dunk tank. People kept lining up and paying their money to the cash-taker. Afterward, Sam put a towel around my shoulders and said, "You done good. The fair sponsors told me the dunk tank did the best business of all the stalls at the fair."

"Gawd, didn't think it possible, but I even enjoyed it."

"I knew you would," she said. "You can be yourself when you want to be. You should keep at it."

20

With the coming of the new year and no football or All-State banquets, I had to search for things that kept me connected. I had told the Emissary that there was more to this most American of sports than simply the playing. Everywhere I turned, people asked favors, wanted me to tell them how it felt to win, and encouraged me to apply my talents in other ways beyond football.

"I don't know how to do hardly any of this," I confided to Sam.

"You don't really have to do anything if you don't want to," she said. "Still, you can't hide under a toadstool either. Then you get to be like me and you'll be disparaged and cut off."

"I think sometimes you cut yourself off...intentionally."

"You're probably right. I sorta thrive on being a crank. You, however, can't avoid putting yourself out there. You matter to people, and they're going to want to know more about you and what you're going to do next."

"I guess I get nervous, or...or even angry about what they're asking of me. I can't really tell them since I'm not always sure."

"So, pick and choose. You're smart enough to figure out what matters."

I did some of the things Sam suggested. I played in a twenty-four-hour soccer game to raise funds for autism research (I had to read up on what autism was). I joined a hiking club where people of all ages took weekend excursions on demanding mountain trails to scenic water gaps.

Mr. Fasciola even got me into an American history club where we met after class to discuss the Civil War and important Supreme Court decisions, and how the first black president got elected. We each chose a topic and had to make a presentation. I did a talk with slides about the "Greatest Game Ever Played."

I'd read about it as part of Keysiana prep courses. The so-called greatest game was between the New York Giants and the Baltimore Colts in 1958. The contest went into overtime and was said to usher in the wide popularity of pro football among American fans. I liked it because a wide receiver like me, Raymond Berry, caught twelve passes for 178 yards.

Most of the other students considered it "lightweight" on a historical scale. "Don't judge prematurely," Mr. Fasciola told the doubters. "The Budweiser Clydesdales have sold a lot of beer. Last year, almost 129 million people watched the Super Bowl. I'd consider it symbolic of America's competitive spirit."

I did all this to maintain contact. Football players couldn't just play football. I was learning slowly that there was more to life than what I once thought could be a cocoon that I never had to leave.

I found supposed history nerds that I could talk to. They told me to read Mark Twain, Steven Ambrose and Laura Ingalls Wilder. I went on hikes into the outback with people who studied rock minerals and traced old Indian trails. They didn't even know I played football, although many were impressed when I proved inexhaustible in climbing a thirty-degree slope.

I insisted that Sam come along when I took a school-sponsored trip to the Smithsonian Museums of American History and Natural History. I was fascinated that Americans collected so much of their past and the nature that surrounded them and put it in one place. What really caught my attention was a display of meteorites. I stood at attention as I peered into the glass cases with the mounds and chunks of ancient iron and stone and said to Sam, "Do you ever wonder what else resides in outer space that we should explore and learn from?"

"You think scientists will tell us?" she said. "It'll only upset us."

"Oh, we should brace for any revelation. It could change our lives," I replied.

* * *

When I wasn't hiking or learning about history or traveling to expand my horizons, I often went to the track after school to work out, to stay in shape. It gave me a certain peace to be there alone and jog or walk. Sometimes a few other students would hang around and kick soccer balls on the field or locals would toss Frisbees to dogs or run the steps of the stadium.

On cold days when I could see my breath clouds forming as I walked rapidly around the tartan track circling the field, I'd get the urge to take off and run the full oval. Four hundred meters, as fast as I could.

What did Ladarius and the coaches clock me at in the 40-yard dash? Three-point-nine seconds. Faster than anybody has ever done it.

I'd asked Coach Dan to smuggle me a stopwatch. Lad had told me the Olympic record for the 400-meter was forty-three seconds. Sometimes I clocked myself in under forty. Once at thirty-eight. I told no one because they might not have believed me. Yet I knew what I could do and knew that my speed was a gift. The Keysians knew it, cultivated it, and gave it to me to use at my discretion. I didn't abuse it. But when a few of the Callister Cascades football games were on the line, I brought it out of the shadows. It was my secret weapon that I sometimes chose not to keep secret.

One day, when it was bitterly cold in the depths of winter, the stadium and the track oval were totally empty. Or at least I thought so.

I ran a few sprints to warm up. My legs felt like pistons, my feet like the turbocharged rockets that Coach Sawyer boasted about. Suddenly, I heard the echo of footfalls coming hard behind me. I turned and found a kid in an ill-matching sweatsuit, wool cap, and ragged running shoes. He was doing a more than decent job of keeping up with me.

"You sound fast," I said as he practically ran up my heels.

"I am fast. Not as fast as you, but dang fast for my age."

"What is that... your age?"

"Eight going on nine."

"Why are you following me? Nobody's usually out here but me in this weather."

"Oh, I know who you are. You're Sublimious. You played with my brother. I saw every one of your games during the season."

We then started walking side-by-side, our breaths mingling in the frigid air.

"Who's your brother?"

"Kadeem. Kadeem Nabors. He's a wideout like you."

"Oh, yes, a very good player. Very athletic. I learned a lot from him."

"Yeah, but he didn't like you. At first, I should say. You stole playing time from him. I tell him, 'Why not...you the game-breaker. He not.'"

I had to laugh at his honesty. I wondered if Kadeem laughed. I doubt it.

"What's your name?" I asked.

"Kairo. It means victorious in Arabic. Your name, Sublimious, I like it. Nobody got a handle like that. It's very individual. Matches what you are."

The kid was not a *kid*. He was very poised. We spoke like equals.

"Kadeem finally like you, you know. He thinks you helped our team beat teams they might'a shouldn't beat."

"Yes, probably, although I could never say that. My friend Ladarius told me to be humble. It's part of being a good teammate—let your actions speak for you."

Kairo was not shy. He told me exactly what was on his mind.

"You know I play football. Bunch of us after school. On Saturdays too. We play pickup. Most are around my age. All colors, man. No discriminatin'. Even got a couple Indians from India and a Korean."

"It's something, isn't it?" I said. "How great it is, just to play?"

"Yeah, we rock each other. Some dudes are better than others. Don't tell them that. Like you say, action speaks. No flexing or zackin'."

"Don't you have a league?" I asked. "Like some kind of youth league?"

Kairo shook his head. "We don't much like having adults around. Besides, not that many adults are interested. They got their own stuff to do."

I wasn't used to talking with kids this young. But I had a feeling that Kairo had sought me out for some reason. He wasn't just running to keep up.

"You know I had to learn to play," I said. "From coaches, from teammates, from your brother. Doesn't Kadeem ever come out and show you how to run a pass route like he ran in a game?"

"Ah, not hardly ever. He got things on his mind. He's thinkin' 'bout going to college next year. If he can get a ride somewhere, maybe for his gymnastics."

We kept walking briskly. It was cold, and we were blowing on our hands even though we both wore thin gloves.

Then we started running again. Kairo was really fast. His form was upright, legs and arms flowing in a smooth synchronization. His breathing was steady and calm. I could picture him running his own pass patterns, just making them up instinctively.

We ran a full oval, backed off for a short jog, then ran the oval even faster. I didn't run it flat-out. Kairo matched my pace. I was impressed.

Neither of us was breathing heavily when we stopped.

"How often do you play—pickup football like you say?" I asked.

"Two days a week after school. Most Saturday afternoons."

"What if some of us on the team came out and played with you and showed you a few things that we learned? What if I get Kadeem and Ladarius and some others?"

"That'd be decent. But I don't think Kadeem will come. I asked him before."

"Well, it can't hurt to ask again. You're fast—that's a start. How're your hands?"

"Oh, I can catch. Last pass I dropped squealed like a pig."

"Squealed, eh? Then you knew it had hit the ground."

Kairo turned to me and we bumped fists. "You know I watched you all last year. Stood in the stands and cheered 'cause nothin' ever come to Cascades like you and the rest of the Rams. Don't know how you did it sometimes, but you did it, man."

I blew into my gloves and smiled. I never much thought about a boy like Kairo Nabors cheering in the stands at what I did, what his brother Kadeem did, what Prince and Ladarius and Stew Shavers and our whole team did.

But that was part of why I had come. To find out what it felt like for football to have an impact on Americans. Even in its smallest towns, in places where almost everyone paid attention and cared.

I could tell Kairo cared.

And now maybe I—*we*—might think about doing more for the Kairos of Callister Cascades. We brought them a championship, but maybe we could go beyond that. We could give some of their caring back.

It sounded like some deal Sam would get me into, for my own good. *For your growth, like the dunk tank*, I could hear her laughing foxily. But all I had was a hazy idea. Maybe it had to sit in the back of my mind and ripen.

21

SAM KEPT TRACK OF EVERYBODY WHO "WANTED A PIECE OF ME." THAT'S how she put it. At the beginning of the week, she'd give me a folder full of print-outs from Instagram, TikTok and WeChat, of posts, likes and follows. There were plenty from school, from local businesses, and from those who thought I'd make a "great influencer."

She said that after a while, the flow started to drop off. "Once your name disappears after football, it ferrets out the uninformed and the disinterested, and a lot move on. Still, there are some who want to party or take selfies with you or think you should run for class president."

Then Sam said there were definitely contacts I should at least explore. One outfit called Alpha-Dorse had been after me for weeks. She had been holding them off while the air cleared after football season.

"You need to spend a little time being a regular person, not a personality. There are too many attention suck-ups in this world. Best to let them fade off into their black holes."

"What's this Alpha Dork? Is it something I should bother with?"

"It's a company that tries to sign emerging high school athletes to endorse-ment deals. The representative is named Sid Boniface."

"Endorsement deals—what's that all about?"

"You'd get paid to say you wear some brand of jock shoe or drink one of those sugar-fueled energy drinks."

"Who cares whether I'd wear a shoe or drink a drink?"

"Apparently, somebody would, and Alpha-Dorse would give you money to lend your name and maybe image to some brand."

"My gosh, who would know me? Sublimious Clancy from Callister Cascades. Nobody's ever heard of me outside of this town."

"Well, I think this Mr. Boniface knows that," said Sam. "He says you're not high-profile yet, but he's keeping track of you. He's identified you as a potential star who could very well break out next football season."

Sam always tried to make me face what she called reality. She was convinced I was always skirting the edge of it. "You're not even half aware of how famous you could become. I mean, look, you made All-State, and nobody even heard of you before you started playing this past year. You're on the radar of people in the know, just like this Mr. Boniface says."

"I'm only in high school. You mean this man can give me money at my age?"

"Guess so. It's the companies that give you the money. You wear their jewelry or talk about them on a social media channel, they'll pay you."

I was confused. This was another facet of football and American sports that I didn't see coming and that I had to contend with. I didn't play a game for the fame or the money. I didn't want to talk to this Mr. Boniface. He sounded like someone who could tie me in knots as he tried to shape my future.

Sam gave me looks that she said were her special trademark looks. *You can't be innocent forever! What do you want from me? Do I have to hold your hand on everything?*

She wasn't being mean. She was my defender. At times, she simply threw up her hands and thought she should let me wander off a cliff to see what it felt like.

"Listen," she said, "I hear you talk with Mr. Fasciola occasionally. Maybe you should ask him for some advice. He'll tell you straight."

* * *

So I did. We set up another lunch. This time the menu was takeout Chinese. Spring rolls, Kung Pao shrimp and chicken, steamed dumplings, and fried rice.

"Chinese isn't filling," he said. "You can go work out this afternoon, or whatever you plan to do. And I can stay awake in my one o'clock class."

Sam had given me a printout of the Alpha-Dorse proposal that Mr. Boniface had sent to her. She also better explained it to me. Some forty state high school associations in the United States agreed to allow their students to sign NIL agreements with businesses to say they used their products.

I still didn't know why anybody would care whether I, or some other athlete, would wear certain sneakers or eat at particular restaurants. But Sam said one seventeen-year-old, a baseball player who was going to be the number one pick in the Major League Baseball draft, could make hundreds of thousands of dollars in endorsement contracts. Mr. Boniface wasn't going to offer me anything within a million miles of such a deal, but he was touching base with me in case I had another "blockbuster year" in football next season. Then I'd be a "hot commodity."

"See what Mr. Fasciola thinks," Sam recommended. "Should you even listen to a guy like this, who apparently has money to throw around?"

I sat at a desk. Mr. Fasciola sat behind his big bureau, eating with chopsticks.

"I've been following your journey, Sublimious. Who would've ever thunk it that first day we met in homeroom? I remember thinking you didn't look like much of an athlete, but you assured me that you had the powers that would prove me wrong."

He deftly lifted a cube of sweet-sour chicken between two slender sticks. "You took us to the Class A championship, made All-State, and went to the governor's gala with Samantha Schneider of our homeroom. Quite a ride."

"Yes, I've been fortunate."

"It's good to have a friend like Samantha," he said, dabbing his beard with a napkin. "I was surprised she became your intermediary. She doesn't seem to engage much with others."

"She's been my friend from the start. I was never much at mixing beyond football. She clued me in on things I should be aware of."

"Sort of like a broker or liaison?"

"I guess, whatever they are. She tells me the truth."

"You've put your stamp on this school and town in a limited amount of time," he said, tapping his carton for another bite. "You haven't played football much before, from what I can gather. You became good, better than good, fast. I don't exactly know how. Perhaps you don't even know. People beyond here have noticed, and many of them think they've discovered a diamond in the rough."

I ate slowly. Kung Pao was very spicy. I swallowed with care. "Sir, I'm not sure about the diamond reference. I'm just a little suspicious of all the energy that swirls around my football performance that I never expected or asked for."

"Like this approach from Alpha-Dorse and Mr. Boniface? And Sam even tells me some very prominent college coaches want to meet with you and try to convince you it would be worth your while to join their football program."

"Yes, that sounds right. She doesn't tell me everything," I said.

"Well, let me be blunt. It's the way the world of big-time sports works these days. If you play again next year and become even more of a force than you were this year, these high-powered folks will pursue you with a vengeance. It may be confusing. You may not like it. But they're not going to stop. You'll have to deal with more than a few Mr. Bonifaces. They will all want to sell you the best deal going."

The chicken and shrimp crunched in my mouth. I leaned forward and said softly, "Mr. Fasciola, what if I decided not to even play football next year?"

His dark eyebrows raised. "Why would you do that?"

"Most of my friends are graduating. Ladarius, Aurelius, and Kadeem are leaving. Prince won't be throwing me his exquisite passes any longer."

I couldn't tell him my complete dilemma. I might not be here much longer. After having scoured the field of American football and its many dimensions, I might be recalled when the Emissary thinks I have observed enough.

"Well, to not play next year would be most unconventional. You're too good a prospect. Coach Sawyer will certainly want you back. College recruiters will come after you and shower you with all sorts of incentives, not to mention a lot of money."

"Money to play football? That's not why I played. I came to Callister Cascades to learn the game. I became good at it, very good, many people think. I didn't do it for money. That means very little to me."

Mr. Fasciola remained quiet for a long minute. He drank the homemade root beer and fiddled with his chopsticks.

"Sublimious, I don't know what to make of you. Maybe you're an altruist or just a complete subversive?" he said, sort of chuckling to himself. "You've played yourself into a position that any other young man would give his eyeteeth to be in. Some college coach, or a lot of them actually, will watch you next year, and if you improve, they'll knock each other over to promise that you'll be an important cog in their Top Ten program."

I looked up from my knife and fork and asked, "Is that what I should want?"

He leaned back, his chair squeaking. "It would seem like someone your age would be all in on that kind of prospect. But I like it that you're not sure. You're not programmed like too many of the driven athletes today."

I felt Mr. Fasciola was a good listener, so that I could say almost anything to him.

"Sir," I began, "it seems like football here at our school was the right size this past season. I arrived at just the perfect time. We played together and defeated teams we weren't supposed to. I personally did things nobody else did. That got a lot of attention. Maybe that's as good as it's going to get for me. That might be what I call my apex."

I paused to make sure I had my thoughts in order. "I love it here. I learned as much about football as I could possibly learn. Now I think I have other possibilities. Even with football, there are other directions besides going to a college where a coach sees me helping make it a success. With this Alpha deal, I have no desire to make a testimonial for something I would never use."

Mr. Fasciola opened up his laptop and seemed to begin searching. "You could even study history, God forbid! You could go on an archaeological dig. I plan to do one this summer, and I might be able to secure a slot for you. I'm looking at a list of programs that my old university runs for high school students, where they'll find summer internships for someone like you with your curiosity."

I leaned back and stretched. "I don't know if they're the kind of things I'm after. I do know football has opened up a lot for me. It has started me thinking. I'm grateful for what you, Sam, and a few others have shown me. Now I've got opportunities beyond what my body and feet and acrobatic impulses have given me."

"Well, they're your safety valve. They won't let you down. You can always be sure that there's an Alpha-Dorse and a Mr. Boniface out there ready to monetize them and dial up your shot at fame."

He bit into what he called a fortune cookie. "But you don't seem inclined to march to their drummer. You may surprise us all. Good for you."

22

I CONTINUED TO GO TO THE TRACK EVEN IN INCLEMENT WEATHER. Without football, I came to think running was the only physical activity I had left to blow off steam. I liked my classes, but after a while, I'd look down at my feet and see them dancing without any music. I had to give them an outlet.

On many days, Kairo Nabors showed. Sometimes he'd climb down out of the stands like he'd been waiting for me.

"What time do you get out of school?" I asked him.

"Three. Every now and then, I cut out early."

"They don't catch you?"

"Man, I think the teachers would cut out too if they could."

We'd be on the track even in light rain or snow. I had a waterproof-lined windbreaker with a hoodie. Kairo only had a tattered sweatsuit. One day, I went into the athletic department's clothing bin and found him an old yellow slicker with a wool liner and told him to keep it. He promised to pay for it. I told him I didn't think anybody would ever miss it.

We ran sprints and rested. Then did full 400-meter ovals as fast as we could. He trailed behind by no more than ten yards.

I asked, "You still playing pickup football with your buddies?"

"You know it. It's how we stay out of trouble."

"How many guys usually play?"

"I don't count. A whole bunch."

"Well, is it ten? Twelve? Twenty?"

"I'd say between ten and twelve most days. Some dudes won't even come out in a drizzle. I tell 'em football is an any-weather sport."

"Do you have steady quarterbacks? Others go out for passes or play line?"

Kairo laughed. "You jokin'? We intra-changeable."

"Do you have a regular field where you play?"

"Not always. Sometimes at the Knights of Columbus, where they do have a league, but not this time of year. Other times, we find a Little League field not being used or just a plain old open park in the neighborhood."

"Who brings the football?"

"I got one that's all taped up. Cody brings one his brother used before he went off to the Army. Once we hijacked a ball old cats been usin' playing semipro."

We jogged a lot just to stay warm. I told him, "You know I bet I can get a decent ball from Coach Sawyer if I ask him nicely."

"Could we keep it? I'd take it home and stick it under my bed."

"Don't see why not. Coach may understand that you guys are his future."

"Yeah, there's an older dude, Levi Perez, who got a gun for an arm. He's around ten or twelve. We tell him he the next Prince."

"Whoa, he must be good then."

"Got others, too, who self-love themselves to death."

Kairo never hung around for long. We'd walk and run together for about a half hour, and then he'd take off, saying he had to meet somebody or do an errand for his mother. He explained he didn't have a father, but there were occasional "uncles" in his home. He had to pick up medicines or buy groceries because his mom worked two jobs. He mainly saw her on Sundays when she took him to church.

I wasn't sure how to converse with an eight-year-old, so Kairo did most of the talking. He shared a few stories Kadeem had told him about how the Ram receivers practiced hard and worked together.

"He used the saying 'Shock the World,'" remembered Kairo. "Kadeem like that 'cause it put him a few steps above the Opp. Teams didn't know what hit 'em."

I asked him if I could come to watch him and his friends play sometime. "I have a friend, Ladarius. Your brother knows him. He taught me to play. Taught me the rules of how you work together to be the best you can be. He'd maybe come too, if you wouldn't mind."

"I don't got no problems," said Kairo. "I'd have to ask the others."

"Don't mean to interfere. We could show you some pass routes, only if you're interested. Otherwise, we'd stay out of the way."

"You show us how you ratchet up your speed?" he said with a grin.

"Don't know about that. Speed may come on you slowly...then suddenly."

"Sounds like witchery. You blessed...or not."

*　*　*

I told Ladarius about my offer. He said Kairo and his sidekicks might be a future generation of Callister Cascades Rams who'd keep the new winning tradition alive. "Bring home another state champs trophy in ten years," he grinned.

But Lad didn't want to intrude on them. He thought they sounded very independent, like they didn't brook adults—even young high school-aged ones—bothering their free-style get-togethers.

When Kairo and I met again, he said he and his pickup partners would be glad to see us. "You show us a few moves. We wouldn't have no 'jections."

He gave us an address and told us to be there around three on Saturday afternoon. It was a vacant lot on the edge of Callister Cascades that looked as if it had once had buildings on it that had been torn down. Now it was dirt with patches of grass and occasional misplaced chunks of concrete or rubber. At one end, the players had run a pipe between two wooden clothesline poles for a goalpost.

"Man, they better kick the extra points and field goals clean," said Ladarius.

"You hit any of those props and the whole thing flies apart."

The pickups had already been playing when we arrived. It was a motley crew, to say the least. Guys in hand-me-down uniforms, in sweatshirts and shorts despite the cold, and in floppy jackets, jeans, and boots. They wore baseball caps, safari hats, wool pullovers, and one tattered cowboy hat.

Kairo came over, and I introduced Ladarius to him. "Sure, I know you," said Kairo. "You were one of the wideouts with my brother Kadeem. Best blocker of all the receivers, he told me."

Ladarius smiled. "Yeah, Kadeem was a good observer."

"Sixteen showed today," said Kairo. "I told 'em you guys were coming."

I said, "We don't want to interrupt anything. You've got a game going?"

"No sweat. I'll call them over, introduce you, let them talk to you a little, and then you lay a few of your moves on us."

Kairo put two fingers in his mouth and whistled loud enough to break eardrums. The players sidled over and stood in a loose semicircle, drinking from water bottles and dixie cups. He said they could ask us anything for about five or ten minutes, and then we'd show them a few routes that we normally ran.

All of them stared silently for a moment. Then a kid in a blue and gold Callister jersey piped up. "You 'spect to win the state championship 'cause most didn't think you would?" There was a sprinkling of uneasy laughter.

"As the year went on, we kept improving," said Ladarius without hesitation. "When we got to State, we thought we had as good a chance to win as anybody."

Another spoke to me. "You got a name like a brother—how'd you get it? You don't even look like us. You got a gold shine."

"Guess it doesn't matter what you look like—you can have a sharp name."

Some laughed; some scoffed.

"How come nobody comes to our part of town to teach us ball? You boys are the first to even bother."

"Did you ever ask somebody for coaching help?" said Ladarius.

"No, we just hook up with ourselves. More fun that way."

"You may have something there. Then, when you get to junior high and high school, you can learn what you need to know from real coaches."

One kid who looked a little older than the others stepped forward. "Hey, by the time we get there, to the organized part, maybe we want to go our own ways."

"That's your choice," I answered. "I didn't start to play until this year."

"Yeah, that strange," the older kid said. "How you do that? Get so good so fast. Some of us think you hidin' in the weeds and then just drop on us like T'Challa getting back his full powers as Black Panther."

I flinched. "Don't know him or his powers," I mumbled.

"We don't neither." He waved a hand above his friends. "He probably wouldn't bother comin' to show us anything. At least you dudes did."

That question came a little too close to the bone, so Ladarius and I decided to show them a few basic pass routes we'd run during the season. We ran combo patterns where we had to complement one another. A crossing slant and quick breakout into the flat, where defenders had to make an instant decision on whom to cover. A corner and a post where we started together, and then suddenly broke off and went deep in opposite directions. A rub-off in the flat where one receiver had to be mindful not to be called for a pick by referees as he sprang the other open.

We asked a few of the players to mirror the routes that we had run. Once, two of them collided in a heap, angrily cursing each other. They ran the deep routes with real enthusiasm and hustle. They had natural skill, and they knew it.

"Us boys can probably make your Rams team right now," one kid joked.

Then Ladarius and I ran what we called the "route tree" by ourselves. Kairo said their best passer, Levi Perez, would throw us the ball. And he did with surprising precision. We did comebacks, hitches, quick outs, posts and corners.

We then encouraged them all to run the routes, and Ladarius and I joined Levi Perez in tossing them passes. We had defenders try to cover the receivers.

Some pattern runners were successful; other times, the defenders came out on top.

We went at it for a good forty-five minutes. It began to get dark before we quit. All of the pickup players gathered around us, sweating and breathing heavy. We knocked fists, and they thanked us for coming out.

"Now we know why you dudes won the championship," one of them chirped. "You had to do some work to get there."

"You keep showing up for these pickups," I said. "If you still like it, then come out for the teams. Coaches need guys who take the game to heart."

The kid who seemed older stepped forward again. "Will you come back? Bring some of your cham-peen mates. Bring that Prince quarterback of yours. He can teach Levi a few things, and then Levi will become him in a few years."

"If that's okay with all of you. We'll get some others."

"Yeah . . . yeah, okay with us." Most nodded in agreement.

23

IT HAD TO COME EVENTUALLY. I WAS SURPRISED THE EMISSARY HAD taken so long. Maybe it was Leadership's way of giving me every opportunity to experience as much as I could of American football—playing it, learning its intricacies, running the gauntlet of challenges that came afterward. Mr. Fasciola called the enormity of possibilities woven around the game a "web of wisdom." You either mastered as much as you could or you got swallowed up by both the large and small details.

I suppose I was ready to meet our Leader, but I had some trepidations.

I was summoned to the safe house. It looked even more primitive than I had remembered it. The floor was faded wood, the walls whitewashed, and the ceiling had one turning fan to keep some air circulating. A single lighted bulb in a lamp without a shade sat on a rickety table. My chair that had once been padded was now a hardwood rocker. At least it generated some movement.

Greetings, Sublimious, how long has it been since the end of football season and that championship you so prized?

"I believe two, going on three months, sire."

Have we given you enough time to pursue the other aspects of football you so ardently desired to explore?

I sat stoically in my seat. I thought rocking might be a little too carefree. "I'm not sure I will ever understand it all. I learn something every day, every week. About people who want me to do things because I was successful. About the opportunities I'm offered. About difficult questions that I must learn to deal with on my own and with the help of generous guides—"

I could have continued, but the Emissary interrupted.

Yes, yes, we watched you from afar. Frankly, it could be tiresome. Watching you go to exclusive dinners with that dominating girl of yours. Being dropped into a vat of water so you can seem more human. Meeting with young boys who all want to play football like you when they get older, and yet we know they cannot.

I was stopped cold by this response. It sounded peevish to my ears.

"I'm sorry you see it that way, your Eminence. It is all part of the learning experience that comes with the game. I believe that was part of our agreement: that I explore all angles so that we appreciate how football infuses the culture.

Well, I suppose, the Emissary said almost reluctantly. *Those sessions with the young boys. We'd rather you come back to Keysiana and hold them with our youth so that they acquire basic skills if they ever have to penetrate this new world.*

There was something about the disembodied voice sweeping the room that struck me as strange today. It wasn't as commanding and all-knowing as I had come to think of it. Perhaps I had been living in this new environment too long, and I was hearing the old voice differently now.

"It can't hurt to pass on our skills to another generation, whether it be Americans or Keysians. I see it as payback for how I've been helped by my teammates. It is one of the most invaluable lessons I learned in my time here."

I sensed a slight buzz above me, and I didn't think it was the small whirling fan.

Perhaps, Sublimious, you have become too close to your new friends and colleagues. Have they come to mean more to you than those you left behind?

It was confusing, this overtone of doubt. I had never heard it creep into our

Lordship's voice before. "I believe I respect my new colleagues with as much esteem as I did my indigenous people. If certain Americans didn't show me the way, then I'd be of no value in any future resettlement."

I thought I heard a rumble in the walls. Some plaster filtered down from cracks in the ceiling.

Your teacher warned you of dangers, did he not? Of high-powered coaches seeking you out and landing on you with vengeance, I believe he said. Of deals if you let them use your words or face. Of showers of money, American money, which will be worthless in Keysiana. Is this what you stayed for, to see what America can offer that Keysiana cannot?

"Sire, they are the choices that those who play sports well in America have to make. Many players take them if they think it makes their lives better. Others refuse if it means they have to give up their freedom or be put in uncompromising positions," I explained.

The Emissary was silent for minutes. For some reason, the fan in the ceiling stopped, and the bulb in the lamp began to blink.

Sublimious, the Powers have given you substantial leeway to pursue your segment of American life. More than most of our other explorers were given. You, of course, will be granted a proper amount of time to disengage. You will return with your wealth of information and insights. Our Board of Collection and Clearances will debrief you, and our people will honor you for your great sacrifice. You've completed your service. It is time for you to come home.

I heard a long exhale. The Emissary had made his final declaration and was anxious to cut off all communications before I could respond. I felt anger building inside me. I began to rock in my hard-backed chair. I rocked as if I might carve my protest into the rough-hewn floor.

"You may retreat so you cannot hear *my* final statement, but I have one," I said into the void.

"The Powers may want me to do what solely benefits their purposes. Others, my friends and guides, give me the freedom to make up my own mind. I have learned one important thing here in America: I have choices.

"I GET TO DECIDE!"

24

My return to Keysiana was set. At least in the single-mindedness of the Emissary and his sovereigns. I knew I had pledged at the start of this journey to examine an alternative way of life. Yet was this the only way? My lone choice? To go back to a society possibly teetering on the brink of extinction?

My Liege did say I had an undefined amount of time left. I vowed to make the most of it. I was not only a Keysian explorer, but I was an explorer here in my present world. I had more choices, and I was determined to learn as much as I could. Sam said there was one college coach who insisted that we meet.

"He's famous," she declared. "Declan 'Deke' Dempsey. You ever heard of him?"

"Yes, sure," I faked. "Watched his team on TV about a dozen times."

"Well, you probably did. But you didn't know his team from the Little Sisters of the Poor. You just studied the plays like some high-tech visionary."

"Didn't his team's uniforms glow like the face of the sun?"

"They might have. All the teams change their uniforms every week, so Nike and Adidas can sell the new variations like different flavors of Pop-Tarts."

"How do I see Mr. Dempsey?" I asked.

"The Division I recruiting rules say that he can visit juniors in high school once off-campus. So he can come here to the school if he has permission."

"We should tell him to come then, shouldn't we?"

"Sure, we can. But I'd make certain that Coach Sawyer knows. Maybe Coach would like to meet him. It would be quite a feather in his cap to know one of his players was being courted by the top coach in America."

I asked Samantha to set up the meeting.

When she did, she said his liaison was surprised that Sublimious Clancy had his own agent already, a fellow high school student, no less.

I said, "Did you tell this person that I don't make any big decisions until I consult with Sam the Slam?"

"No," Sam replied, "I only advise. You're your own boy-man."

When we told Coach Sawyer that Deke Dempsey was coming for a visit, he nearly choked on his dentures. "Comin' to little ol' Callister Cascades? To see Ob-livius, the player I developed to such a polished gem? Did he say if he needed a thirty-third coach on his staff?"

The visit was hush-hush around the school. Mr. Dempsey arrived in a tint-ed-window Mercedes-Benz with a driver and an assistant who was a bodyguard. He was a large, impressive man who had a glow about him like his team's uniforms.

When Mr. Dempsey disembarked, Coach Sawyer was first to greet him. "Coach Deke, it is an honor for this little ol' peckerwood to meet the greatest coach since sliced pumpernickel. We been running your spread-read-option forever."

Coach Dempsey looked him up and down and said, "We ain't run that for at least two years."

He shook hands with a small welcoming committee, including the Cascades principal, and then said to me, "Where's that gal of yours? She sure takes care of you like a mama grizzly!"

I introduced Sam. "You wanna job after graduatin', honey? How about ridin' herd on our blue-chippers who get lost finding the one class they gotta attend?"

Coach spoke with what Sam called a good-ol'-boy twang. She thought it was a pretense.

We went into a teacher's break room with nice, soft couches. The school cafeteria staff had laid out pastries, fresh fruit, and a pot of coffee. It was just Coach Deke and me seated in a private huddle.

Coach said his scouts had put him on to me and had him watch some film. My acrobatic moves and speed had bowled him over. He wondered how I had developed such a unique blend of skills. "You can't put that stuff in a Cuisinart and have it come out in a superstar frappé, can you?" he asked.

Sam had counseled beforehand, "Let him do most of the talking."

Coach Deke said he wouldn't beat around the bush. College football had become a free-for-all recruiting circus. But he was putting together a stable team of outstanding athletes coached by the best staff going. His school had the most lucrative NIL collectives and pools of house money.

"And the kicker," he said, "is I've signed the best young high school quarterback in the country. I'll have him for at least three years, God willing. I want to pair him with the best young receivers I can find. That's where you come in. I know you got another year here in school, but if you commit to me now, I promise we'll have the prime-one passing attack in this big ol' land. I know you'll develop even more in the next year, and then when you come out and join us, it's Katie-bar-the-door."

He was near breathless after he spelled out his vision. I almost asked him who Katie was. "Whaddaya think, Sublimious, you interested in joining the best of the best when they let you loose here at Callister?"

I leaned back into the plush cushions of the couch. "You know, Coach Dempsey, football means a lot to me. I played with a fine quarterback this past year, and I wouldn't mind playing with another one again."

"All you gotta do, son, is sign a little ol' letter of intent."

"I've got another possibility, though. I have a chance to go on an archaeological dig with my favorite teacher. We'd be exploring the origins of the early Clovis people, one of the first prehistoric settlers in North America. That is really what I am focusing on at the moment."

Of course, I did not tell him of my other immediate concern: my return to Keysiana. That would surely short-circuit his brain. But I was interested in how he might react when I took a complete U-turn from his college football sales pitch.

"Whoa, boy, most of our main recruits train year-round. A lot go to developmental camps to keep the edge honed."

"Yes, I understand, sir. Truth is, I love history as much as football. If I were to ever choose a college, I'd look at its history department before its football program."

"Well, son, that's your prerogative," said Coach Deke, standing and stretching his large frame. "I'm gonna have to go back and find out what we got hiding in our history buildings. Maybe we got some kinda expert on these Clovis gents."

"I must be honest," I said, "I'm not sure I'll be playing football next year."

Coach Deke stopped chewing his pastry. "Yo-dad, that'd be a downright shame. I might be able to find you a hedge-fund alum who'd give you a little sweetening sugar to help you in your decidin'."

"I'm glad we could meet." We shook hands. "Your team seems like the place to be if all you want to do is play football."

"You got that right. We practice it and teach it and dream it twenty-four hours preseason, in-season, and postseason. If you just strap it on for the game, that's pretty much an anticlimax. That'll be a little bitty pillow fight. Football is our religion."

We walked out to the school atrium, where Coach Sawyer and Sam were waiting. Coach S proposed that Coach D come back and watch a game one Friday night. "We'll turn Ja-len-limious loose to do some fancy-dan pigskin pickin'."

"Well, you take care of him. He's a gem who could make history."

Mister Dempsey turned to me once more before climbing behind his blacked-out car windows. He waved. "You change your mind and choose to come with us, we'll plot your life for you, so the only thing you gotta do is pick a wife when the time comes."

Sam looked at me strangely. "You two discuss your marriage plans?"

25

I KNEW I HAD TO GET THE THINGS DONE THAT I WANTED TO GET DONE before the decisive moment came. For starters, I owed a few people who had become my guides and close friends a final goodbye and profuse thanks. However, I wasn't really adept at one-on-ones. That's what I liked so much about becoming absorbed in a team. You had to mesh so many brains and bodies to reach a positive outcome.

And like Sam always told me, I was *only* original on a football field. Off it, I needed a seeing-eye dog, a detective to check out danger zones, and a tough-minded micromanager to steer me to the right path.

Fortunately, I had Sam, whom I'd met on the first day in homeroom. I had Mr. Fasciola, head of that homeroom, who sold me on American history and set me straight over assorted luncheons. And my friend Ladarius, who laid out the "rules of the road" so I wouldn't stick out like a nine-inch nail.

I had to do one last thing with them, if it came to a final farewell. The one tried-and-true meeting place I always felt comfortable in was the Drakos restaurant. Big Niko said he would make something special, the best dishes he remembered from the old country, where his mother taught him to cook.

I would pay him whatever it cost. Explorers were given funds every month that were far from extravagant but enough to stay a step ahead of American inflation. Nico Drakos tried to wave my offer away. He'd made plenty betting on our games. But I insisted on paying; I didn't want Ladarius to even have a hint I knew of his father's wagering.

We gathered late, at a table specially set in the rear of the Drakos. I asked Sam to wear the same dazzling outfit she wore to the All-State banquet. She refused. She said she had to maintain her tough gun moll disguise, otherwise classmates would start to think she was approachable and even sociable.

"It's only Ladarius and his dad, and they already know you're a pussycat," I said. "Mr. Fasciola, too, and I suspect he knows you're my goodwill ambassador."

"Nah, I need people to believe I carry a sawed-off shotgun in my backpack."

She came in a sweatshirt advertising the WWE wrestling federation (a salute to her mother), a leather fringe skirt, and men's scuffed work boots. She'd also borrowed her mother's shrunken-head earrings to go with her black skullcap.

Mr. Drakos said, "Sam, you're a walking daughter of Hells Angels."

Mr. Fasciola brought a bottle of top-shelf wine, a pinot noir red. "No school tomorrow, right?" It was a Saturday.

Big Nico laid out the first course. Separate plates of salad with ripe tomatoes, cucumbers, and Kalamata olives, doused with extra virgin olive oil, and a large piece of feta cheese on top. He then set a big dish of yogurt with mint and lined it with fresh-baked sourdough bread for dipping in the middle of the table.

"What's the occasion?" asked Ladarius. "Dad doesn't do this for everybody."

"I just wanted to bring the people together who helped me the most in my first year at Callister Cascades," I said, raising a piece of sourdough for a toast.

The others held glasses of wine or slices of bread.

"Wait, there's something else going on here," said Sam. "I can tell. After six months, I can read Sublimious like the back of my hand."

"You mean the one with the black rose tattoo on it?" laughed Big Nico.

"Something's up. I feel the mini-heads on my earlobes tingling," said Sam.

"Can't I express my gratitude to each of you for being helpful in football and in regular life?" I asked. "I was new, and you all showed me how to fit in."

"But you always had an ulterior motive, whether you admitted it or not. And you've got one now." Sam was always a pesky mind reader.

"Well, I didn't want to tell you this. It's not 100 percent sure," I lied. "I may not be with you much longer. A critical point in my life has arrived, and I may have to leave. I felt it was important to give you a warning and not simply disappear."

Sam, Ladarius, Mr. Fasciola, and even Big Nico all seemed startled.

"When will you know?" asked Sam. "Might this happen in the next day? Or week or month?"

Mr. Drakos was dispensing the next course. Pastitsio, a baked pasta-like dish with a rich ragu of ground beef, tomatoes, and spices in the middle with a béchamel sauce on top, baked to a golden-brown crust. It smelled delectable.

"No exact date. I don't want to leave, but it's a commitment I've made."

"To whom?" Ladarius probed. "What did you promise? A year in our town, so we won the state championship?"

"Do you really think that's why I came?"

"I don't know. You showed up out of nowhere. You never told us where you came from. You've got a skin tone that's between white, black, and brown. You had a take on life and football like none of us."

I dipped a slice of bread. "You hardly ever asked about any of that. You gave me the freedom to be who I am."

Mr. Fasciola cleared his throat as if he were about to state a historical fact. "I, for one, thought you were strange from the beginning. But, my God, someone who loved history and asked questions as much as you did, I was just glad to reach out to you. And now you're going to mysteriously leave. It's a pity. I'll miss you."

I sank my fork into Big Nico's Greek pasta. It was about the best food I'd had in a long time. "You know, when I arrived, I hardly knew anything about football. Ladarius and my teammates and coaches showed me everything I needed. Sam didn't care who I was, and I didn't care who she was; we just clicked. Mr. Fasciola made me understand that the history of this country

mattered. You all made me over in six short months, but now someone—
some very important someone—is asking me to come back. I can't tell you
why because I do not think you'd understand."

Big Nico pulled up a chair and sat down. "You could try telling us. But you're
right, I think. It's likely beyond us."

Sam had been intently quiet for too long. "Sublimious, you're the only person in the whole school who treated me like I was somebody right from the beginning. I needed that...needed you. And now you're going to take off on me—us?"

"Didn't you ever make a promise and then it sort of ties you down?"

"Maybe, I dunno," Sam stumbled. "I want you to be different."

"Well, I'm sorry, but I'm not. I'd like to be strong and say I can't leave. I
won't leave. The decision to go or stay gnaws at me. I just don't think I'm able to
renounce my promise."

I looked at the faces around the table. Brows were wrinkled, mouths tight.

"If we can't change your mind," said Big Nico, breaking the tension, "let's
have dessert."

He rose, and he and an assistant brought out a custard pie he called *galak-
toboureko*. It had several layers of thin filo pastry filled with custard, baked in
an oven, and the instant it came out, it was soaked in sweet syrup and cut into
squares. They served it with small glasses of the "wine of St. George" to wash it
down.

We all ate silently with our fingers until they were gummy-sticky.

Mr. Fasciola held up his tiny glass in salute. "To Sublimious, he's gotta do
what he's gotta do. We won't stop him, but Coach Sawyer and this town sure are
going to miss him. It'll be like Haley's comet passing through on its way to the
next galaxy."

I did a double take. My teacher didn't know how close he had come.

I then turned to Ladarius and said, "There's one more meeting I'd like to
keep. With Kairo and his pickup players on that old weedy field. Do you think

we could get all the wide receiver brotherhood together and go do something with them?"

"Sure, some day this week after school. You still going to be here?"

"I'll guarantee I will."

* * *

Ladarius rounded up all the wideouts except one of our bench players on a Wednesday after school. Prince even agreed to come, despite working with a trainer full-time, so he could compete to become a starting quarterback at a Division I college next fall.

I coaxed Coach Sawyer to give us three brand-new footballs to donate to Kairo and his crew. "They may be your future," I bribed Coach. "I think they have the makings of another championship team."

We met them on a cold, windy afternoon. Sixteen showed up again, outfitted just as ragtag as before. The brotherhood was not impressed with the pockmarked field they played on. "Jeez, you could eat a rusty beer can if you got tackled on this turf," winced Styles.

Kadeem came, Kairo's big brother. I could tell Kairo looked up to Kadeem by the way he hung with him. Everybody milled around for a while. My teammates spoke about how it felt to win a championship and to be respected by an entire town. They asked the younger kids how often they played and why they weren't in an organized league.

"We like it that way," said Kairo.

"You should have older folks who know what they're doing teach you a little something," Aurelius said. "You know, it's called learning proper technique."

"Didn't you learn to play jus' by playing?" one kid said.

"Yeah, sure. But you'd be surprised what the old ones know."

After we talked, we started to just throw balls around. Prince gave the younger passer, Levi Perez, some tips, and then they threw passes to all the young guys running their own stitched-together routes.

Kairo whistled, assembled everyone, and broke them into separate groups. Each of us—Aurelius, Styles, Kadeem, Ladarius, Heath, and I—took a few and demonstrated the primary pass patterns we had learned from our coaches.

The young guys listened raptly and ran the routes with enthusiasm. They razzed each other when they freelanced or dropped a pass. A few of our wideouts threw the passes. So did Prince and Levi Perez. Prince admitted that his young protégé might be able to make the high school team right now.

Kairo came up to me after about fifteen minutes and suggested we play a pickup game like he and his friends did on a normal day. So after arguing about who made the fairest teams, we divided up into eleven-on-eleven and marked out goal lines and sidelines with coats and hats.

We chose to play two-hand touch, figuring that the ground was too much like a minefield to risk playing tackle. Prince was one quarterback and Levi Perez the other. One team called themselves the Mountain Goats and the other the Bighorns as variations of our Callister Cascades Rams.

The Goats and Bighorns went at it hot and heavy. Aurelius made a circus catch over the middle and got clocked by one of the young guns. "Yo, man, this *touch* we playin'," he bitched. "No crackin' a man like he a can a corn!"

"Oh, you soft," hollered back Styles.

Kadeem went deep for a high-arcing pass from Prince, and Kairo stepped in front of him, snatched an interception, and ran it back for a pick-six. Everyone swarmed him for high-fives, including his brother, who had a huge smile on his face.

I was on Levi Perez's team, and in our huddle, he told me to go long and make one of my patented moves like he'd seen me do during football season. "Oh, no," I shivered, "Ladarius will yell that I'm showboatin'."

Levi Perez snarled, "Who cares what Ladarius thinks? You're on my team now, we goin' for the whole enchilada!"

I smiled at the kid's audacity. I knew immediately that he was Prince's heir apparent. He was already cocky and absolutely sure of himself. So I couldn't refuse. I ran the route. Did a spin and a flip as I came out of my cut. When I snatched the pass and crossed the goal line, I did a cartwheel and topped it off with a two-legged split.

Oh, geez, oh, gawd! I held my breath. I knew what was coming. Ladarius hovered over me, held a hand out to give me a lift off the ground.

"Aren't you going to yell at me?" I recoiled from him. "No hot-doggin'. Come on, read me the riot act!"

He looked at me, an eye winking. "Can't tell you that anymore. Story's changed... Sounds like you're on your own now."

We played for a good solid hour. It was cold and growing dark when we stopped. All of us came together in the middle of the tortured field and bumped fists and said, "Good game. We'll do it again, okay?"

Then Kairo came up to me and grabbed me by the elbow. "You gotta come back. All you guys. Turn us into a team. Get us into some kinda spring league. Don't know where or how, but you and your mates will know. You're the friggin' Callister Cascades Rams. You're the champs. You can be our coaches."

I draped an arm around his shoulders and hugged him. He smelled like sweat, the hard-effort kind that I had gotten used to during football season.

"I'd like to come back," I said. "I'd give anything. You're going to be a one-of-a-kind receiver, better than me. I'll even let you borrow some of my flair."

"I can learn those shake-and-bakes," smiled Kairo. "I'll even match your speed someday. You gotta work with me. All you guys need to turn us into a team that can be your successors. Then the Rams make a name for themselves forever."

I shook my head. "Don't know if I can, Kairo. I'd like to, honest, but you've got your brother and these other brothers. They'll show you how."

He held me tight and wouldn't let go. "Not like you, man. Not like you."

We hung on to each other. We both sensed something was about to happen bigger than both of us. But eventually, we parted, and Kairo went and joined Kadeem.

When I left, there was nobody else around. I gazed up into the cold night sky and swore it couldn't end like this. Games where everybody felt alive and cared about each other were too beautiful to end so totally.

26

THE HEAVENS GREW DARK. IT WAS THE LAST CLASS OF THE DAY. I looked out the school windows and saw large black nimbus clouds boiling to the west. My classmates thought it was an early spring thunderstorm about to arrive, but I knew it was a portent of some core change in my life.

Earlier, I had been called to the safe house in the Gates of Wisdom Forest and informed that this was the day. My day of departure.

It was not the Emissary's voice I heard. Nor the Oracles or even my tutors. It sounded like a recording telling me to prepare to leave. To bring nothing with me. I was to exit the way I had entered—only myself in street clothes. And I was to tell no one that I was returning to Keysiana.

The voice was stern. I had the feeling that my time in America had suddenly been cut asunder and that I had no alternative. I couldn't protest, bargain for more time, or see if another arrangement could be made.

I was told to be standing in the middle of the Callister Cascades football field, shortly after dark. The vessels coming for me would slowly appear in the night sky. I should stand stock-still so that their searchlights would find me.

I watched the storm building out the windows. I thought of it as an omen. Swirling winds arose, and torrents of rain began to pound the school window-sills. Flashes of lightning and booming cracks of thunder shook the building. The fearsome weather heralded this as more than a normal day.

I saw Sam after the final school buzzer sounded. We sat in the cafeteria as the storm raged outside. We shared a bag of Cheetos and drank Gatorades.

"You couldn't leave on a day like this, could you?" smiled Sam. "In the middle of a gully-washer."

Sam had always been clairvoyant. She could read my mind like no other. "I'm afraid this is it... the day," I said glumly. "My last day in Callister Cascades."

"Must you really go? Can you refuse, say 'No, I'm not leaving'?"

I took a swig of Gatorade and watched the wind-driven rain pelt a large windowpane. "I could. You see, I've not told you the truth. I am not who you think I am. I've come from far away and I've promised to go back once I've learned everything I needed to learn."

"Learned about what?"

"Football and how it fits into America. I came with a special gift, and I applied it. I helped this school win a championship, and this town believe in itself. As I did, I began to fall in love with this place and the friends I've made. I've found I have choices. My choice is to stay, but it is not that easy. They are coming for me, and I don't know if I have the will or the power to resist going."

"My God, where are you going? Where are they taking you?" asked Sam.

"Far. Farther than you can even conceive."

Sam swept a hand across her brow. "And they're coming today?"

"Yes, tonight. First thing after dark."

Sam reached out and grasped my wrist. She asked, "How can I help you? If you want to stay, what can I do to keep you here?"

"I don't know that there's anything you can do. You're strong—the strongest individual I've ever met. But it may take more than your power and wisdom to get things done... to help me overcome what I've pledged to do."

Sam shuddered as a thunderclap broke over the school and shook the windows. "I will think of something," she said as the thunder receded. "You'd be surprised what I can do when I put my mind to it."

I knew if anyone was able to challenge the power of the Emissary, it was Sam.

I didn't know what she had in mind, but she had three hours to plan it.

"When are they coming?"

"Around six. Just after dark."

"Okay, if you really want to stay, we've got to join forces. We've got to believe in each other."

*   *   *

The thunderstorm had passed to the east about an hour before six. The air was now cool and crisp. The sky had gone from a hazy gray to an intense blue to a starry black. I had stayed in the building after school was finished and went up to Mr. Fasciola's homeroom. He kept an assortment of history books on a shelf in the back of his room and had given me a key to enter whenever I wanted.

As the hour of rendezvous approached, I was so nervous I could barely read a word. I kept glancing at the large clock on the wall. I wondered how my Keysian patrons would come. How would they make their presence known? I knew they had the technological capabilities to seek me out and retrieve me quickly and stealthily.

At quarter till six, I arose and began walking through the school hallways. Everyone was gone—the janitors, the springtime sports players. I didn't even see any of the maintenance staff who came in and cleaned at night.

I made my way through the athletic meeting, locker, and shower rooms to the tunnel that led out to the track and football field. The stadium was ghostly quiet. The large light standards towered above the stands like dark giants.

I walked to the center of the field as I had been ordered. I wore only running shoes, jeans, a sweatshirt, and a Callister Cascades High School varsity jacket zipped tightly to the throat.

I could hear myself breathing. Sharp, brittle, anxious breaths.

Then, faint lights began to appear in the sky, moving very slowly out of the north. About five or six separate lights silently crept in above the stadium, hovering above the empty stands. Their bright beacons reached out and rotated above the field as if searching for the one profile that would tell the seekers that they had reached their destination.

Suddenly, most of the dark ship-like silhouettes backed off, then one of the lights grew in intensity and dropped down over the edge of the stadium. It crept in slowly like the drones I had heard about. The single black outline dipped closer. Its strong spot bathed me in a ring of light.

A deep metallic voice emanated from behind the blinding beam: *We have come a long distance, and the stars are aligned for your return. Are you ready to come with us, Sublimious Z. Hormats?*

At that very moment, Samantha Schneider emerged from the stadium tunnel and walked briskly out onto the field. She stood beside me in the glow of the ship's flooding rays. She was dressed as she had been for the All-State banquet: spectacularly glorious. She firmly grasped my hand and stared unflinchingly into the light.

I began my reply with a shaky voice as Sam squeezed my hand tighter.

"I have spent more than six months in America. I have learned about football as the Powers required. I have fit into life here with great interest and passion. It has been a privilege to explore another culture and to sample all of its range of options."

Yes, that is all well and good, came the unswerving voice from above. *You were sent for a reason. Now the Powers who have dispatched this Recovery Fleet want you to come aboard and not dither.*

I stood defiant. "I must tell you more. I have made a friend here who taught me the rules of the road. How to humbly use my special gifts at exactly the right time. How to love the buzz when your moment of excellence arrives."

I didn't know what to expect, but I knew Sam would pull off something that matched my building sense of empowerment.

Then out of the tunnel came Ladarius. He walked briskly and stood stoutly across from Sam on the other side of me.

My voice gained in strength. "There were my fellow receivers who shared playing time with me, even though I was the newcomer. They did it for the good of the team. We became a brotherhood that believes in each other."

Across the field strode Aurelius, Styles, Kadeem, Heath, Bottoms, and Murphy.

Prince followed them and tossed me a perfect spiral.

"That's the quarterback who always put the ball exactly where I could catch it. How do you forget someone who knows you that perfectly?"

Now slowly out of the tunnel emerged Coach Sawyer and assistant coaches Tarzan Sampson and Demon Dan.

"Coach never asked where I came from, only if I could play. He never got my name right, but he used me at the most crucial times. He had assistants drill me until my head hurt, literally and figuratively. I cannot leave them behind."

Next came Mr. Fasciola in his dark beard, which did not have the usual flecks of lunch lodged in it. He walked exactly how I might picture Abe Lincoln striding.

"This teacher taught me about America, where it has been, where it might be going, and how it has pockets of meritocracy as well as danger signs I had to watch for. He made me aware of opportunities beyond football that appear just as rewarding."

I didn't know how Sam had rounded them up or even knew of their existence. Kairo and his young pickup players came onto the field in their ragtag outfits and scruffy hats. They shambled across the field with a loose self-assurance.

"These are the young guns who play for the fun of it, who nobody else ever bothered to teach. They need mentors. I can be one, and so can my brothers."

Everyone joined me at the fifty-yard line. My friends and teammates, coaches and teachers, and young pickups. They stood in a long line to either side of me.

"Last but most importantly is my best friend, who has brought all these people together. For all of these reasons, I need to stay. Without Sam—Sam the Slam, as she brands herself—I would have been lost. She made this baffling society understandable and put it at the very center of my growing vision.

"I cannot leave her. I can't leave any of these friends and acquaintances. They have defined a new life for me and given it true purpose."

The light from above became even more intense. It waggled from side to side.

The voice became tinny and strained.

You are breaking your promise, Sublimious? Is this what I must report back to the Emissary? You are renouncing Keysiana and staying in America? If our stress builds, you will not join the other explorers to advise us on how to emigrate to safety. Must I tell Leadership that you have chosen a new life and will not be returning with us?

"Yes, that is my decision. If Keysians must ever emigrate to America, I will be here to welcome them. They can come and find friends and guides as I have. There is more than one answer to resolving their future," I said as my voice began to shake.

"My choice is a difficult choice. But I have become aware that I have a choice. I have friends who tell me when I am right and when I am wrong. I once thought I had only one path to follow. I could never see or challenge the Emissary, the Oracles. But that was blind trust. Here, it is earned trust."

The light in the night sky wavered and then pulled away from the top edge of the stadium. It hovered and then grew fainter.

We are leaving. We have come a long way. The Powers will not be happy. You are on your own. We hope you know what you are doing.

The voice faded. The light dimmed and sat for a moment in limbo as if giving me one final chance to change my mind. I held on tightly to Sam and Ladarius. I felt the two lines of comrades radiating out beyond us pass on their strength to me.

"Whew, I'll have to tell you, Sublim," said Sam. "You are more complicated than even I thought possible. Now I see why."

"Sam, now that you know, we shall be complicated together."

THE END

ACKNOWLEDGMENTS

I wish to thank Gayle Roper of the Tel Hai community for encouraging me to find a professional editor. To that editor, David Aretha, who saw potential in my story. And to Charles Levin, Lily Drew and the publishing team at Munn Avenue Press who brought this story to print.

www.ingramcontent.com/pod-product-compliance
Lightning Source LLC
Chambersburg PA
CBHW060416310726
48976CB00003B/1077